Ponderosa Pines
Days of the Deadwood Forest Fire

by
Annette Gagliardi

illustrated by
Elizabeth Glaser

PP

POCAHONTAS PRESS

DUBLIN, VA

This story is based on actual events of the Deadwood Forest Fire of 1959 and of the Stabnow family's experience as they wait to evacuate. Some say it is brave to fight, and that is true. But it is also brave to be ready—yet wait. The waiting, as conditions worsen, can ask us to be the bravest of all.

Ponderosa Pines
Days of the
Deadwood Forest Fire

ISBN 13: 978-1-955338-07-3

Illustrator: Elizabeth Glaser
Cover Artist: Elizabeth Glaser
Cover Layout: Erica Onsrud
Interior Design: Deborah Warren

Printed in the United States of America

POCAHONTAS PRESS
DUBLIN, VA

POCAHONTASPRESS.COM

Dedication

This book is dedicated to my father, my uncles and other miners, and all the brave firefighters who risked their lives to fight the 1959 Deadwood Forest fire. It is also dedicated to those who wait for the firefighters to return.

- A. G.

The artwork in this book is dedicated to Oscar William Stabnow, Jr. and all the volunteer firefighters who helped get this forest fire under control and extinguished.

- E. G.

Acknowledgements:

Thanks to Mr. Mastel's fourth-grade class of 2015-16 at Kenny Community School, who were the readers of one of the first versions of this story. Thanks also to the Pillsbury Avenue Book Club who were early readers and provided valuable feedback. Thank you to my four daughters, Rachel, Erica, Marian, and Maggie who read, advised me, and edited various versions of this manuscript. My sister Elizabeth Glaser, one of my most devoted supporters and the illustrator for all my books, provided feedback on the content and helped me remember the events of the book. She is also the illustrator of this manuscript. My cousin, Cathy Rufer, also helped me remember details. Thanks to Josh and Lynsey Tjaden and Nick Caple who generously shared expertise about firefighting.

I could not have completed this book without the expert advice and direction from Pocahontas Press. Debbie Warren, especially, helped me from the very first email to the last edit.

Finally, thanks to Tim, my spouse, who supports all my artistic endeavors.

Contents

Map

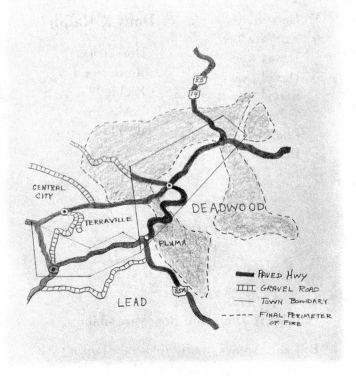

Family Tree

Bill & Anne

Betty 12 yrs
Annette 9 yrs
Lenny 8 yrs
David 7 yrs
Stevie 5 yrs
Valerie 4 yrs
Charlie 3 yrs
Baby Mark 18 mos

Dolly & Ralph

Doreen 9 yrs
Ronny 8 yrs
Richie 7 yrs
Becky 5 yrs
Ralphie 2 yrs

Roger & Jolene

Cathy 9 yrs
Debbie 7 yrs
Mike 5 yrs

Bill (Dad), Dolly and Roger are siblings.

Bill and Anne's family lives in a house with Dolly and Ralph's family in Lead, SD.

Roger and Jolene's family lives in Deadwood, SD.

Family Photo

Here is a photo of our two families with not all the children -- yet.

Back row: Valerie, Dad, Stevie, Mom, Aunt Dolly, Doreen, Uncle Ralph, Ronny.

Front row: Betty, Annette, David, Lenny.

1

First Day of School

Sliding into my desk for Geography, my knees knock against the desk side and I wince. *Ouch. Darn it!* My skirt catches on the space between the seat and the back. Frustrated, I stand up, then smooth the back of my pleated skirt and slide into the desk seat again. I look at the clock. Everyone always seems really excited about school, but it only makes me grouchy.

It's the last class of the day. My wooden desktop has a neat round hole at the top righthand corner which makes me imagine the olden days. I'd be using a quill pen and ink. But, I'm glad for ordinary pencils and pens. I can just see myself getting that ink all over. The initials *TJ + RS* are carved into the surface top and the black wrought-iron sides are peeling skinny slivers of paint.

My teachers have given so much homework, I'll be up until midnight getting it done. Mom won't let anything slide for tomorrow. I sure don't want one more assignment, but Mrs. Johnson will probably give us something to do.

She's just like all the other teachers, thinking their class is the only thing we have to do.

I worry about how much of my evening will be used up on homework and if the whole year will be like this—me hitting the books every night. I look up at the chalkboard that has our reading listed in crisp white letters on one section of the board. Mrs. Johnson has written her name in perfect penmanship. I think about how sloppy my handwriting is, and wonder how much she's going to want us to write. I hope she just wants us to read the book and take the tests, but I know that's wishful thinking.

Why doesn't Mrs. Johnson tell us to go home? That would suit me just fine. I've already got so much homework and the first day of school is not even over yet. There must be something good about third grade. What? What could it be?

I try to think of something positive. I look down at my new saddle shoes. The white and black are so brand-spanking new they almost glow. I smile, a little satisfied, before I remember the teacher and the mounting homework.

I gnaw my pencil's eraser with my teeth, just shy of chewing it clean off, then pull my geography book out of my bag. It's heavy and looks like whoever had it last used it for a football. I rub my fingers over the dog-eared book edge.

Mom is for sure gonna make me cover this book. I hope there is a good brown paper bag lying around some-

where and that I can find enough tape. Sheesh! Another thing I am not good at.

Everyone knows brown, paper grocery bags are the best because they're heavy and last most of the year. Scotch tape is good, but masking tape works better. You can get your friends to write on the cover, or you can doodle all over it, so it's some small entertainment. Still the covering itself is a bit difficult. Mom knows how to fold the edges in to make them slip over the inside of the cover and keeps the paper cover on better. She says we should learn how to do it because "practice makes perfect." The last one I did fell off about a week later. Of course, I had to do it all over again.

Mrs. Johnson has been standing at the doorway. Now she walks to the front of the classroom. She says in a loud voice that gets our attention, "Students! Students! I have an announcement!" She motions for Sally and Abigail to get into their seats so she can continue. Seeing those two together makes me wish for a best friend.

No one wants to be my bestie. No one wants to sit with me at lunch or hang out at recess. I'm a nobody.

At lunch, all the third-grade girls huddled at one table. There was no room left for me to squeeze in, so I had to sit at the "extras" table with kids from different grades. I felt like a big baby. At recess, Sally had her jump rope. All of us girls lined up to have a turn. Then the bell rang. I stood in the line for most of recess and never even got a turn to jump.

Cripes!

My attention jumps back to Mrs. Johnson as she continues to almost shout. It must be important.

"There is a forest fire just north and east of Lead. It is, in fact, at the edge of Deadwood where they are evacuating.[1] You ALL are to go STRAIGHT home. NO dawdling! Go straight home to your parents. Please pack up your bookbags quickly and get your lunch boxes. Then, out you go. And good luck to all of us."

Mrs. Johnson's face is set in grim determination as she steps to the door. My thoughts start rushing as I grab my books and hurry to stuff them into my bag.

Wow! A fire! I wonder how close it is? It must be pretty darned close for them to send us home. I hope Mom is okay. What will happen to Dad, down in the mine? Is the car at home, or did Dad take it today? I hope there is a way out of town!

My books are not sliding in place as smoothly as I hoped and, when I pick up my bag, several books spill out and drop loudly on the floor. My pencil case drops. It opens, scattering pencils, pens and the eraser onto the floor all around my desk.

"You are going to have to get a move on, young lady!" Mrs. Johnson scolds me. "If you packed your books more neatly, they wouldn't spill out like that. And get a zippered pencil case so they are contained."

She comes over and deftly places my books into the bag, then takes my pencil case from my hands and puts it into the bag. Not even looking at me, she closes the bag, hands it to me, places one hand on my back and fairly pushes me out the door.

Why me? That was so embarrassing! Needing help from the teacher! I feel like a kindergartener!

I rush out the school door and search for my siblings. My older sister, Betty, stands waiting for us. Her hair is still as neat as when we started our day. I know mine was a mess before lunch because I went into the girls' lavatory and my reflection told me so. Betty is in the schoolyard standing tall, with her books in her arms. Our brothers, Lenny and David, wave to us and jog over.

"Where were you? We were lookin' for ya'," Lenny says.

"Oh, I spilled my bag 'n had to pick everything up again," I reply, feeling sheepish.

Our cousins see us and call, so we wait for them. Doreen, Ronny, and Richie race over to join us.

"Where's Becky?" I ask, looking around for my other cousin.

"Oh, she's a kindergartener. They start tomorrow," says Doreen.

"I should have remembered that. Stevie is in kindergarten, too. Sheesh," I murmur to no one in particular.

The seven of us (siblings and cousins) trudge home, marching like an army platoon: Betty first, then Doreen and me, Lenny and Ronny, and finally, David and Richie. We walk quickly, quietly, in step two-by-two.

The city warning siren blares—a long single note falling and rising to crescendo, once, twice, three times.

2

A Forest Fire

You might think that seven kids is a lot, but there are more people in my family–lots more. My parents, Bill and Anne, have eight children. Betty, the oldest, is twelve years old. Next is me, Annette. I'm nine and in third grade. Then comes Lenny who's eight. He's in second grade. David is seven and in first grade. Five-year-old Stevie is in kindergarten. The little kids are Valerie who's four, Chuck, who's three, and last is baby Mark, who's just turning eighteen months.

Dad's sister, Aunt Dolly, and her husband, Uncle Ralph, have five children. They are nine-year-old Doreen who matches me, and Ronny who, like my brother Lenny, is eight. Richie is seven and is David's best friend. Becky is just starting kindergarten with my brother Stevie, but she plays with Valerie more than Stevie. Little Ralphie is two. He is younger than Chuck but almost a year older than baby Mark.

Aunt Dolly and Mom have almost matched each other child for child until the youngest. I noticed Aunt Dolly's belly is getting rounder again, so I 'spect she'll have another baby in a couple months. We kids don't usually get in on the "secret" until closer to when the baby is due. Uncle Ralph teases that he and Bill like to keep their women "barefoot and pregnant," a comment that makes Aunt Dolly turn red and slap at him.

Dad says, "We finally figured out what was causing all these kids and stopped." Then he gives a laugh like it's the funniest thing on earth, but I just don't get it. Mom glares at Dad but smiles a little, too.

My family and Aunt Dolly's family live upstairs/downstairs in a large house. It wasn't built for two families but we make it work. All seventeen of us live in this house pretty well together. Here's how we make it work.

Aunt Dolly's family lives upstairs, but they are downstairs with us most of the time. We kids share two of the four bedrooms: we five girls all in one room and the seven boys in another. Each pair of adults has their own bedroom. But baby Mark still sleeps in the crib in Mom and Dad's bedroom, which is next to the laundry and the lean-to basement.

We have even more family living close by. Uncle Roger is Dad's and Aunt Dolly's brother. He and his wife, Aunt Jolene, live in the town of Deadwood, which is about two miles away. They have three children. Cathy Jo is nine. Doreen and Cathy Jo are in the other third grade classroom, so I don't get to see them as much as I want. Debbie is seven and in the same classroom as both David and Richie. Michael is five. We'll see which classroom he goes into. Every grade in our school has two classrooms. Even with that, there are many cousins taking classes together.

We get to see all our cousins a lot because we go to church and Sunday picnics together. The men all hunt and fish together, too. Sometimes us older kids get to go with them to hunt or fish. But, when we do, we have to be really quiet.

All three men work in the Black Hills Homestake Gold Mine. Both Uncle Roger and Dad left at 6:00 a.m. this morning to work the day shift. Dolly's husband, Uncle Ralph didn't go with them because he's out of town visiting his sick mother.

~ ~ ~ ~ ~

"Hey Mom! We're home!" Lenny shouts as all of us kids file in the front door. Mom is sitting at the kitchen table, pen in hand, making a list.

She looks up and shushes us, "The little kids are still sleeping. Be quiet!"

Becky and Stevie have been playing quietly in the under-the-stairs closet where our toys are kept, while the youngest kids sleep. They join us.

"Hey Mom! There's a fire!" Lenny says.

"They sent us all home from school!" Ronny shouts.

"I know. I know. Will you guys pipe down. Dolly and I are organizing to pack the car. We want to be ready to evacuate when they tell us to go," Mom says.

"How 'bout everybody go outside until the little kids are done with naps," Aunt Dolly says as she gets up to look in the cupboard.

We all file back out the door, then Mom calls Betty and me back in to help, and Aunt Dolly calls for Doreen.

I run upstairs to change my school clothes, only to find my younger sister, Valerie is sleeping on my bed. I dress as quietly as possible, but of course she wakes up and starts to cry.

"Hey, Valerie. It's okay. You're okay." I sit next to her and rub her back a little so she will quit crying. She calms down pretty quickly and we just stare at each other for a little while.

"Oh! I forgot. Mom wants me to help her. I need to go downstairs," I tell her. Then, I'm not sure about what to do next.

Should I bring Valerie down with me or get her to go back to sleep?

"Valerie. Go back to sleep, sweetie. It's okay. It's still nap time," I speak in my softest voice. But she has other ideas.

"No. I want to help, too," Valerie says and climbs out of bed. She's four now, so naps are almost a thing of the past. Her fine, sandy-blonde hair falls across her face as she sits up. She pushes it out of her eyes, throws her blanket off, then hops to the floor.

Cripes! This day has not gone like I thought it

would. Mom is going to be mad that Valerie is up.

When we get downstairs, Mom gives me her "I'm-angry-with-you" look and says, "Well, now that you woke up your sister, you can be in charge of her. I had wanted you to help me gather stuff to pack in the car, but now that Valerie is awake, someone will need to watch her."

"Okay, Mom. Okay. I can do that," I say in my most appeasing voice. I sure don't want Mom to be mad at me. "Do we know where the fire is? Will we have to evacuate? If we leave, where will we go? When will we know? Will Dad come with us? Will we wait for him to come home from work, then go?"

"You ask too many questions! I don't know. I just don't know! We'll have to wait until they tell us to evacuate," Mom says, sounding exasperated. "Just take your sister outside and keep an eye on any of the other little ones who come out."

"Yes, Mom," I call back and take Valerie by her little hand. She is still pretty tiny for a four-year-old and compliant enough to willingly take my hand as we head for the door. Then she pulls back for a moment and cries, "I have'ta go potty!"

"Well, sure ya' do. Let's do that 'afore we go out." I lead her to the bathroom just off the kitchen and, for a change, I'm patient enough to wait for her to finish.

Once we are in the front yard, which is mostly dirt except for one almost-grassy hill, we settle near the older boys who have not bothered to change from their school clothes.

The boys are gathered under the giant pine tree that stands on the north edge of our yard. Richie is up in the limbs of the tree and the others are craning necks to see him and calling advice to him about where to place his feet and hands.

"Another one being talked down?" I ask Lenny who is standing next to me.

"Yeah. He got up pretty high, though."

Mom steps from the kitchen door and calls out to us, "Annette! Lenny! Please go water the garden. Let me remind you that it's a very hot day and you can get water from the faucet anytime you want. The plants rely on the rain and us for their drink. I really do want the garden to keep producing food for this family for a few more weeks."

"But Mom!' Lenny says, whining a little, "The fire will just burn everything up anyway. Why do we hav'ta water?"

"You do not know if the fire will reach us or not. Hopefully there will be something to come back to when the fire has burned itself out. Just do what I tell you and get the job done." I haven't said anything, yet I get sucked into Lenny's scolding, as Mom gives us both a stern look, then goes back inside. Sheesh!

The day is blazing hot—the kind of day that can only come in late summer or early September, when the grass has had a couple weeks to dry and the air is not as moist as earlier in the summer. The fall harvest is arriving and plants everywhere are drying out or dying off. I don't know why Mom is so concerned about us keeping the garden watered. Nights are supposed to be cooler in September than in August. But this year September is starting out like a blast furnace and even the nights have temperatures that make a person sweat unless you are just standing still.

"Lenny, you go first an' I'll second you," I say quickly.

"Oh! Okay," Lenny says as he kicks the dirt in disgust.

I called it. He's got to take the first shift. Still, he knows I'm impatient. He won't have to wait too long for me to take my turn.

I see Aunt Dolly's full, red head nodding to some music through the kitchen window. She is up to her elbows in hot water. The last of the canning equipment is soaking in the suds, and she will have it all in the dish drainer before you know it. I see Doreen standing close to Dolly and accepting the wet dishes as Dolly hands them to her. I'm glad to be outside watering instead of in the hot kitchen doing dishes. When Dolly pulls the last batch of jars from the boiling water bath, there will be two dozen quart-size jars full of tomatoes. She and Mom have already filled eighteen jars and these last six will complete their canning for the day. I agree with Mom that those filled jars look so pretty setting on the counter cooling. Mom says they are a comfort to see because it means we will eat during the winter months. I wonder if we will leave them on the counter or try to take them with us when we evacuate. It would be a shame to see them go up in flames after all the work put into them.

I think about all the other canning that Mom and Dolly have done. I remember the rows of canned apple butter, chokecherry jelly, corn, pickled beets, and dill pickles on the basement shelves. Over the last month, we kids have helped with the canning by cleaning, chopping, and packing food into jars.

All those jars will just blow up if the fire gets to the house. That will be a big mess to come back home to.

Lenny calls me over to take my turn at the garden and I take the hose from him. A short while later, while I'm watering the garden, (a task that I do not mind as much as I let on) I notice the pillowy smoke growing along the north edge of town.

I can smell the burning trees! How close is the fire, anyway? When will we leave? Will we even get a chance to leave? What if we are surrounded by the fire and stuck here!

I can see a haze rising and moving slowly over the northern horizon. Tears spring to my eyes as I realize that the forest will be as dry as everything else. No one goes out to the forest to water. It's probably burning up really fast. Our lilac trees have brown, shriveled up leaves and are looking pretty weak. Yet, Mom doesn't tell us to water them, nor the apple tree that sits next to the south end of the porch. She says there isn't enough water for everything and the garden is "priority," which I think means more important.

The long rows of onions and green beans have been watered. I move the hose to spray the tomatoes and the cucumbers that climb the fence. I'm amazed Mom hasn't asked me to gather more vegetables, so we can take stuff with us. I might just share that thought with her later. Of course, if I do, there will just be more work for me.

The huge chokecherry tree sits on the other side of the fence. A full half of its branches dip into our yard and hang almost to the ground with the weight of their abundant fruit. I drizzle some water next to the lower trunk to water the roots closest to the tree, keeping an eye on the kitchen window. If Mom catches me watering this tree, she'll have my hide. Our water for the neighbor's tree! Especially since he is so vehement about it being *his* tree and we should keep our mitts off!

My cousin Doreen walks over to me. She picks up part of the hose and moves it along, so it doesn't crush the green bean bushes.

"Thanks, Doreen," I say and we stand there together for a while. "I don't even know why we are watering the garden if it's gonna get burned up anyway."

"School sucks!" she says, ignoring my comment. "My teachers gave me too much homework and it's just the first day!"

"Yeah. I know. Mine too!" I reply. "You're right. It does suck."

"Mom made me help with dishes right away and, now, I gotta get myself over to the porch and watch Ralphie 'til supper. An' lookit' the boys, playing like they ain't got a care in the world! Boy, it sure is fun to be a girl around here," she mutters sarcastically, and then trudges off.

She's right! Us girls gotta do all the work and the boys get to play and play. It's just not fair!

"Hey, Lenny. Your turn to water!" I call and hold the hose out for my brother. At least he can share in the work load.

Cripes, he did his turn first! Boy, I must be losing my brain to forget that so soon.

I turn off the water and roll up the hose, winding it around the hook attached to the house. Then I remember I'm supposed to be watching my sister, too, and I look to see Valerie playing in the dirt with one of the four big trucks we have. One is almost new, a yellow Tonka truck that is metal and pretty sturdy. There is a blue Tonka as well, but it only has three wheels. Then, there is a homemade wooden truck that has four wheels, but all its paint has come off. And last, there is a smaller metal pickup truck without any wheels. Valerie has the coveted one with all its wheels, but Charlie comes out and gets it from her easily. Pretty soon baby Mark and our cousin Ralphie join them and life is good, since the number of kids and trucks matches up. Doreen and Becky are leaning over the upstairs porch railing, gazing at the little kids below them. They will help me keep track of the little kids who can get pretty rowdy, especially when they want to do what the big kids are doing.

Betty joins me in the yard and we get to talking as we watch the little ones play and the bigger boys at the tree.

"I wonder how soon we will evacuate from this fire," I say.

"Hmmm. I wonder too," Betty replies. "Mom is getting ready to pack the car, so I think she is planning to go. She'll be calling me back in pretty soon. She's taking a break to think and smoke a cigarette."

"But, where will we go?" I ask.

"I don't know. And I don't think Mom knows either. Maybe they will tell us when the evacuation is announced. I hope they do it before all the roads out are closed off," she says, almost to herself.

"What about Dad? I don't want to leave before he gets home from work. Well, I want to go, but I want Dad to go with us," I say.

Even though the siren has sounded, we don't yet know exactly where the fire is, nor how close it will come to our home. We can see the smoke, so we know it is fairly close and to the northeast. Thinking about the fire, and if we will run away from it, makes goose bumps jump out of the skin on my arms and my neck. The palms of my hands feel sweaty. And, I feel scared for Dad. I wonder if he even knows about the fire down in the mine. So, I change the subject.

"Summer should NOT be over yet! Look at how hot it is still! How can we even think of doing homework in this heat? It was just the first day of school, for heaven's sake, and I got lots of homework already. Why do the teachers think we need homework on the very first day? I know Mom will make us do it right away after supper. Heck, she'll probably make us do homework in the car as we are driving away! It's still daylight 'til about 8:30, so we shouldn't havta' go inside, anyway," I complain, warming up to a rant about how unfair life is.

I already miss the laid-back feeling of summer when a person could wake up whenever they wanted and think about what to do each day while crunching cereal or munching a piece of toast. Even though Mom and Aunt Dolly gave us chores, we still had lots of play time. The summer that has only just ended feels miles away, and next summer seems like a very distant light at the end of a long, narrow, and difficult tunnel.

"It's just not fair!" I finish with a huff.

Homework is so hard for me! This coming year will be hours and hours of homework. I go over and over things but they never seem to stick in my brain. Then Mom will make us do chores, and, after that, there won't be time to play, or watch TV, or relax.

Betty considers an almost opposite thought. "Well, I'm anxious to get to my homework, especially the new science book, which looks so interesting. I want to just sit down and read it through to the end! I wonder if I'll be able to stand going the slow pace of the class, or if I can just read ahead and go back to work with the class." She is thinking out loud and not really even talking to me.

"Yeah. I think I'll just read ahead," she decides. "And, you know, we learn all kinds of stuff in school that we don't learn during summer, so I like school," she says turning to look at me.

"Yeah, of course you like it. You're so smart! You always get As." I stick my tongue out at Betty as I finish talking.

"Well, you're smart, too, Annette," Betty retorts. "You work hard and you get pretty good grades."

"Yeah. Well, no one seems to know that 'cept you!" I retort back, knowing how hard I work on assignments.

As the boys' talk gets louder, we turn and walk to the pine tree to see what is going on. We see they are just horsing around, so we stroll back toward the house. Mom calls to us to help her again.

Valerie comes with me back into the house to see how Mom wants us to help. She's listening to the radio. I stand transfixed, as we hear about the fire so close to our home.

The trash burner at Hillcrest Manor in Central City
was the origin of the forest fire.

Ponderosa Pines: Days of the Deadwood Forest Fire

3

Packing Up

"The fire started about one o'clock in a trash burner, behind the Hillcrest Manor in Central City, on Highway 14A.[2] A piece of burning paper escaped from the burner and lit the meadow on fire. From there, it quickly spread to the forest," says the announcer.

He's reporting on the fire's beginning and is out of breath, but I still recognize Joe Schmitline, "The Voice of the News," on the radio station Mom and Dad listen to.

"The forest patrol at the Deadwood watchtower spotted the smoke and alerted the fire station. In addition, a neighbor next to Hillcrest spotted the meadow on fire and called it in.

"Fire and rescue squads from Deadwood are fighting the blaze behind the Hillcrest Manor. Fire companies have been called from the towns of Lead, Spearfish, Custer, and Sturgis. The Forest Service has set up a fire checkpoint on Main Street in Deadwood, in front of the Franklin Hotel. Recruits from Ellsworth Air Base have joined the fight.[3]

"The wind is whipping the trees and grasses around in gusts of up to forty-four miles per hour," he continues, "It has been forty-two days without rain and today's temperature of 96-degrees holds no hope for any rain. And . . . I am sorry to say there is no rain forecasted for the near future.[4] The fire has just recently jumped Highway 385. Those living in Central City and Deadwood should begin to evacuate, especially you folks on the east side. Other folks in nearby towns, get ready to go in case the fire spreads in your direction, as well.[5] We will keep you posted. This is Joe Schmitline, The Voice of the News, here in the Black Hills, signing off from KDSJ Radio."

Harry, the regular DJ comes back on the air and puts on 'Crazy' by Patsy Cline. Feeling more scared than ever, I block out everything I've just heard and begin singing along with Patsy.

I sound pretty close to Patsy and know all the words. I'm pretty crazy most of the time, so that must be my theme song.

The phone rings and Aunt Jolene is on the line. She and Uncle Roger live in Deadwood.

"Hi. Jolene!" Mom says. "Okay. Yes. I heard the call to evacuate Deadwood. There are buildings on fire?! Wow! Be careful! You are going out through Lower Main Street to Sturgis?[6] Why not take 85A? It's a faster route. Someone came around to tell you to leave town? That's the direction the patrolman directed you? Well, you'll have to go east a fair way before turning south, then. Uh-huh . . . Uh-huh. That sounds like a great idea. No, we're still packing . . . and waiting for the word to go. The authorities haven't told Lead to evacuate yet. I hope they come around to tell us, as well. Harry Daniels is keeping us pretty well informed, but listening to the radio seems iffy. Yes, the kids are pretty antsy. We'll be ready, though. Yes. If we go, we'll meet you in Rapid City. Where? Oh. At the Armory? Good. That's a good enough place. Good luck!" Mom says her "good-byes" and "be carefuls" before she hangs up.

"What did she say?" Aunt Dolly asks, looking worried and wringing her hands a little.

"They are leaving now. The smoke is so dense they are coughing. Jolene could hardly talk. She has the kids in their car and made the quick phone call to let us know. She said she'll call once they get to Rapid City," Mom replies, her voice getting quiet as she talks.

Then, she straightens up and pulls her shoulders back, smooths down her apron and wipes her eyes with the back of her hands. She looks at a list on a half-sheet of paper that she has made.

"Okay. Let's get this show on the road," she looks around at us kids who are standing around her waiting to hear the news. She points to me, David, and Stevie.

"You three kids go into the basement and get that basket of apples we picked yesterday. I was going to make apple butter, but they can come with us for something to eat. Get the two cans of ham and the jar of peanut butter as well."

I walk down the hallway with David and Stevie following me, into what is known as the basement, to gather supplies. In reality, it is another room, a lean-to on the basement level of our home. The room is a walk-out, but we enter from the laundry room which doubles as Mom and Dad's bedroom.

I wish I could make a quick exit into the front yard. It's just twenty feet from this door, but Mom will only call me back. Sheesh. Anyway, I'm kind of scared to go that far into the room, especially when the door is closed.

The dirt floor, the inadequate light, and the dampish, musty smell make it spooky. The door at the other end does not seem as big as a normal doorway, but sheds a helpful stream of light when it's open. It just magnifies the gloom, when it is closed, like today.

We enter the basement. As I walk in, I pull the chain to turn on the single light bulb, which hangs from the ceiling on a skinny cord about four feet into the basement. You can just make it out from the doorway.

I quickly search the shelves that line the north wall for what Mom has asked us to bring. These shelves are stocked with supplies: mostly Mom's canned foods in glass jars, small appliances, and tissues, paper towels, and toilet paper.

"David, can you and Stevie carry that basket of apples?" I ask my younger brother.

"Sure, we kin, a'course," he replies, and Stevie

wordlessly grabs one handle of the basket while David grabs the other. They march out of the basement room leaving me alone to find the other items. I feel suddenly chilly, and hairs on my neck and arms stand up. A shiver races down my spine.

The south wall is hidden in darkness, and, with the other door shut, the room is filled with a deep, inky blackness. "I hate this place!" I mumble to myself.

It's always too dark. The lightbulb is not bright enough. Later in the fall, Dad will hang a deer carcass right in the doorway during deer season. We always havta' get around that naked form in order to get anything off the shelves. If you look sideways, that deer's body resembles a headless human hanging there. It's just creepy all skinned like that, with its muscles and tendons showing.

The memory of that skinned carcass makes me shudder. The room always has a dank smell and I can never be sure what, if anything, is hiding in the shadowy side of the room. One time when I walked in, I stepped on something slimy and screamed. One of my brothers grabbed it up. It was a shiny black salamander. Everyone was all "gaga" over it, but I sure don't want to step on another one. *Yuck!*

I wish I wasn't such a scaredy-cat all the time. You'd think a person would grow some backbone, sometime. There should be a store that sells courage. Maybe they would have a sale so I could afford some.

Continuing to scan the shelves and finding only the canned meat—no peanut butter—I reach up and swing the light bulb, so that the light sways back and forth. It illuminates both sides of the room, but the shadows that were unmoving now jump around, making everything even more distorted. As the single bulb arcs, more light shines onto the shelves. Even so, I cannot see clearly enough to spy the jar of peanut butter.

"Where is it? Where is it?" I mutter. There's a noise in a darkened corner. I shudder and run out of the room fast! I race down the hallway, not even stopping to turn off the light.

"Annette, I want the peanut butter, too," Mom says. "Did you forget or are you just being lazy?"

"Mom, I looked and I couldn't find it," I say, whining a little.

My voice always goes up when I'm scared, but I sure wish I didn't whine.

"March yourself right back in there and get me the peanut butter! It is on the bottom shelf, second section. Really look, this time," Mom says in her sternest voice.

"But, Mom . . ." I protest.

"March! We don't have time for dawdling," Mom says and points her finger toward the hallway leading to the basement.

"Oh, okay," I say in a small voice, then plod down the hallway to the basement room again. I stand at the doorway and peek in, trying to will myself to enter the dimly lit room again.

"You. Are. Such. A big baby!" Betty says right

behind me, making me jump and screech a little.

"You scared me!" I cry.

"I know you're 'fraid of the basement," Betty says. "Look. I'll stand here, and you go in an' git the peanut butter."

"Why don't you get it, seein' as you're so brave, an' all?" I ask.

"You gotta' find courage some time, Annette. Maybe it's on the shelf next to the jelly," Betty says and leans against the doorframe smiling.

"Oh, I thought it was peanut butter I was lookin' for," I reply sarcastically, which doesn't make me feel brave in the slightest.

Trembling, I enter the basement, trying to gather my courage.

Which shelf did Mom say to look? Oh! Here it is. Found it!

I turn around fast and march out.

"Don't forget the light," Betty says. I groan, take two steps back in and stretch to grab the light chain. Pulling the light chain, I quickly make my escape.

"You big wuss," Betty whispers in my ear, but she puts her arm around my shoulders and gives me a sideways, big-sister hug.

4

Seeing the Fire

Meanwhile, the fire grows with each passing minute. The forest is so dense that sunshine through the smoke creates only a veil of light in many areas. The ground has little grass, but there are pine needles, pinecones, and low-growing, shade-loving plants. Ferns and mushrooms compete for the soil nutrients with Aspen, Fir, Larch, and a variety of Pine trees. The mountain range is predominantly Ponderosa Pine, which is why folks call it a Ponderosa Pine Forest.

There is a thick spiral of smoke on the northeastern horizon that has been building since we came home from school. Now, there are visible flames licking the sky as well, and Lenny is the first to spot it. He is quick to run to the tall pine tree and climb up.

"Hey, you guys! I can see the flames from the fire. It's over there!" And he points through the tree branches like everyone can easily see what he's looking at.

"I want to see! Lenny, come down so I can get a look!" Betty says. Then she adds, "Please." She impatiently motions for him to come down.

Betty climbs up quickly to what looks like the very top of the tree. She looks out over the houses to the north. The land is terraced. Each property line has a rock wall lifting one yard from the other. The next house is a ten-foot drop, so Betty has a good view over the roof of the houses. There is, indeed, smoke curling up from the forest. She can see the flutter of flames and a shudder runs through her body.

Because she is twelve years old, Betty knows better than the rest of us the dangers and the possible loss of life that a fire so close will mean to us. She wonders how much more information Mom has gotten about the fire, and she climbs down the tree to find out.

I am going to go up, too. Wait. Maybe not. That tree will sway and bend. What if it bends over so far it breaks? What if I just fall out? Ugh! I'll climb it another day.

I follow Betty into the house as David attempts to climb the tree once again.

How will Dad find us if we evacuate? Where will we go when we leave? Will our home burn down? I just can't imagine what it might look like. Where will we all live if this house burns up? How will Mom, Aunt Dolly and all us kids fit into the car?

"Mom, how are we gonna' get everyone of us into the car, when we need to leave?" I ask as we enter the kitchen where Mom and Aunt Dolly are getting food packed into a cooler.

"Yeah," says Betty. "Even though we are masters at cramming people into the car, will we be able to all fit? Aunt Dolly, her kids, and all of us kids—that will be thirteen kids and two adults. How will that work?"

"Well, some of you kids are small. We can do it," Mom replies. "We will just have to."

"But, Mom. You are filling up the way back, so there won't be any room for the boys to sit back there," I continue. We have a station wagon, and the boys usually sit cross legged, in the back area that doesn't have a seat, but now she has had us fill it with food, blankets and clothing.

"We will seat you big kids in the back seat, and every big kid gets a smaller child on their lap," Aunt Dolly says. "There will be room for everyone. We can put a couple smaller children in the front seat with your mom and me."

"Here. Fill up these jugs with water and put them in the back of the car, please," Mom says as she hands me two empty milk jugs.

The fire siren sounds again, its single note rises to crescendo then decreases three times, in one lonely voice like the wail of a small child. I cover my ears. All the other kids cover their ears as well. We all look at Mom and Aunt Dolly with our eyes full of fear.

"Alright you kids, settle down. Even though the siren has sounded, we do not yet know how close the fire is, nor how close it will come to our house, or even if it will get this far. We only know it is burning the forest north of Deadwood and parts of Deadwood itself," Mom says and wonders out loud if Dad will be home at all tonight.

Ronny says, "That's about two miles away, or maybe one mile."

"It'd be 'bout a mile and a half," Lenny corrects him. They jostle each other a bit and Mom tells the boys to go outside if they are going to rough-house.

A niggle of worry grows in the back of my mind. I remember that the miners sometimes get called to fight the forest fires.

"What if Dad has to fight the fire? What will he wear to keep from getting burned? How will we find out about him? Will they give him fire-fighting stuff?" I ask, looking to Mom and Aunt Dolly.

"If your dad and Uncle Roger get called to fight the fire, they won't be home anytime soon. We will just eat a quick supper and be ready so we can leave when they announce it," Mom says and the grim look on her face lets me know not to ask any more questions. I turn back toward the sink and finish filling the jugs with water.

In fact, the men will not be home all night, nor tomorrow as they fight one of the largest and most destructive fires in Black Hills history. Early that morning, Dad and Uncle Roger saw each other briefly as they rode the elevator down two, then three levels into the mine. They went into different tunnels and when the siren blew, came up with other miners. Still, an immediate thought for both men was of their families and each other. They are brothers and friends.

The siren signals the men to come up from the lower depths of the mine. They all know the drill. The evacuation of the mine, in case of cave-ins, fires, or other events is drilled into the men. Gathering teams to fight forest fires, flooding, and other natural disasters is practiced regularly. Still, practicing and drilling is drastically different than the actual going.

"Grab your gear! Hang on to your helmets and tools. Let's git to gittin' as soon as possible," the foreman shouts as he points. "All you men on my left will get on that bus. The rest of you move over and get on that second bus. This fire is just north and east of Deadwood, so we are gonna' divide and conquer. Some of you will work the north fire and others will go to the eastern front," he continues.

As the foreman moves to speak to the bus driver, he shouts over his shoulder, "Good luck to us all!"

The first bus leaves just as the last man steps onto it, before the doors even close. The second bus leaves just as urgently.

Dad and Uncle Roger get a glimpse of each other as they are sent to different buses. They raise a hand in acknowledgment, then move as quickly as they have practiced.

Dad can see dense smoke billowing skyward like a giant thunderhead. In less than five minutes of riding the bus, they approach the northern edge of the fire line. Dad can see the tops of the trees glowing with a crown of flames that color the forest yellow and red. He can smell the burning wood and grasses. Bits of flaming debris float like snowfall through the air, fall onto the forest floor, and ignite instantly. He takes a deep breath to settle his nerves and braces himself for the work he knows will be required to put out this fire. He says a silent prayer that they can keep the fire from their homes and that no one loses their life.

As the bus slows, Dad puts his miner helmet on his head, picks up his shovel and lunch box. He bravely steps from the still rolling bus. The intense flash of heat is like someone opened a giant oven door. Dad begins to sweat immediately.

Harry Daniels was the radio station owner and deejay.

5

Harry Daniels

Mom and Aunt Dolly go to the radio and listen intently. Harry Anthony Daniels, owner and deejay of KDSJ, has been providing updates about the forest fire. His radio broadcast is the favorite channel many families listen to all the time, including ours. One big reason is that KDSJ can be heard all around the mountain area while many other stations are blocked in one way or another.

Harry Daniels starts talking. "It's another hot one here on the Ponderosa, and that was Guy Mitchell feeling sorry for us with 'Heartaches by the Number.' That number, for you listeners, is NINE-ty FIVE smokin' degrees! YessireeBob, the thermometer has reached another ninety-degree day! You're listening to Harry Daniels strokin' the smokin' stacks on KDSJ. Here's another golden record from Elvis, who tells the weatherman, 'Don't be Cruel'," says Harry.

KDSJ plays country and western music, jazz, show tunes, the weather, farm reports, and news. There is something for everyone. After his time in the Army during World War II, Harry moved with his brother to Deadwood where the radio station was started in 1947.[7] Mom and Dad are absolute loyal fans and won't even entertain the thought of turning the radio to another station.

Suddenly, the airwaves go silent as the radio station's transmitter goes dead. Mom goes over to the radio and fiddles with the knobs. Then Aunt Dolly goes over to check the electric outlet. She pulls the plug out and puts it back in several times, which does nothing. Mom keeps turning the knobs. Finally, they both stop in exasperation.

"Oh! My goodness," Aunt Dolly says looking at Mom. "I bet the radio station has been impacted by the fire. You know it does sit on the north side of Deadwood."

Mom looks at her, shakes her head, then she grabs her inhaler from her pocket and sucks in a swallow of asthma medicine as she breaths. We all sit for a minute just looking at the silent radio.

"How will we get the news? What will we do if we don't know when to leave? Are we gonna' stay here and get burned up?" I ask, tears beginning to well up in my eyes.

"Will we be burned up?" Richie repeats, his mouth gaping wide. His eyes mirror the "O" of his mouth.

"Of course not!" Mom says severely. Then she takes another puff from her inhaler. Then she presses her apron smooth and starts again. "The main thing is to not get all worked up about it. We'll turn on the TV and see what the news has to say."

Lenny rushes over and turns on the television. The "Sam Levenson Show" is on KOTA, Channel 7. It's a talk show that we kids never watch because it's boring and because there's no action. Anyway, Mom says it has adult themes, which means there's some talk she doesn't want us to hear.

Aunt Dolly goes to the television and turns the knob to change the channel. Not even one channel is broadcasting about the fire. She leaves it on Channel 3, KRSD-TV, which has the end of a movie, on Movie Matinee. We kids sit down and watch, transfixed. Aunt Dolly says the station will break into the program for any news of the fire.

The phone rings and, after listening a few seconds, Aunt Dolly says, "Here. Let me hand the phone to Anne. She owns the car." Aunt Dolly hands the phone to Mom with a scared look. Mom takes the phone, listens, nods, and presses her lips together.

"Yes. Yes. Mae, I understand. Well . . . if it comes to that. Yes, of course we'll take you. No, don't worry about it. I know you do. Yes, I know. We do, too. Okay. That's for sure. Well, don't worry. It'll all turn out fine." Mom sits down while she listens some more.

Mae is the lady in the house just north of us, in the step-down space we see from the pine tree. She is single and has fourteen kids, although some of them don't live with her anymore. It has always been a mystery to me how she has so many kids and no husband. She gets food from the county, and Mom swaps our venison for her 3-pound cans of peanut butter and Spam. The large chunks of Spam Mom turns into "Sunday Ham" by adding a mixture of brown sugar and mustard and then poking whole cloves into a pretty pattern and roasting in the oven. Mom adds a pound or two of margarine to the peanut butter to make it spreadable. I remember how hard that peanut butter is to take out of the can and how Mom beats and beats it to make it smoother.

Finally, Mom hangs up the phone. Aunt Dolly looks at Mom with a question on her face. Mom just rubs her head. They sit and stare at each other for a while and the little kids go back to watching television.

"Mom. What's going on, now? What did Mae want?" Betty quietly asks.

Mom says, "Mae doesn't have a car and wants a ride out when we go."

Aunt Dolly shakes her head and goes to the sink, then pours a glass of water.

"Well, we already have a full car. How we gonna' add her? Plus a bunch more kids?" I ask. Packing another adult and another dozen kids into our car seems impossible to me.

How will we all fit? Will the tires hold all that weight? Will we get arrested for having too many folks in one vehicle? Mom must be insane to say we could take them.

"We can't very well leave them behind to burn up," Mom says in a quiet voice. "Perhaps we won't have to go. Maybe another car will come along or a rescue vehicle will help us. She only has six kids at home right now, so it's not as bad as it could be."

"Yeah, and perhaps pigs will fly!" Doreen says, a bit loudly, so the boys look over at us.

"Doreen!" Aunt Dolly says. "We will do the Christian thing. And, that is to help those in need, as best we can."

"Okay, so one more adult and six more kids. Let's see. That's three adults and nineteen kids. It's a good thing we have a station wagon. We'll have to take stuff out of the wayback, so we can put people in. If we get everyone in the car and there's no food, what will we eat?" I ask as I begin to solve what looks to me like an unsolvable problem.

"It'll be like a grand jigsaw puzzle! No need to remove anything," Aunt Dolly exclaims. "We'll tuck you kids into the nooks and crannies of the car and just drive away! Some of you can sit on the blankets and clothing."

"But, Aunt Dolly, there's only so much room in one car. Really! Even without the food, how are we going to get all of us in there?" Betty says in her most concerned voice.

"Girls, it will all work out, one way or another," Mom says. "We won't need to solve that problem until it stares us in the face. Shush, now."

"Yes. There's room on the top of the car. We'll just strap a couple of you up there," Aunt Dolly says with a smile, "and the glove compartment will hold the baby."

"Oh, Mom!" Doreen says, and marches off.

Betty and I both cross our arms over our chests and silently sit down to gaze at the television. Then we look at each other, because we both know that taking Mae and her kids in our car is not EVER gonna' work.

About a half hour later, the radio starts blaring and everyone jumps. We forgot that it was still on. Mom had accidentally turned the volume way up, so Harry Daniels is shouting at us.

"Sorry for that long station break. We had a transmitter failure when the fire moved across Highway 14A into Boulder Canyon. It burned through some lines, but our engineer has made the repair. I'm glad to be back on the air! We'll stay with you all until the bitter end, no matter how hot it gets," he laughs.

Harry loves being on the radio and really enjoys his time on the air. I think he enjoys being on the air as much as we like listening to him. Now he places a record on the turntable, and 'Mack the Knife' by Bobby Darin flows out over the airwaves.

~ ~ ~ ~ ~

At the station, the phone rings with a blinking light instead of a ring tone. "This is Harry Daniels talking to you from KDSJ," he says.

"William H. Carnahan, Lawrence County State's Attorney, here.[8] The fire is burning Deadwood along the north side of town. It's already burning structures, and moving fast. Please repeat the announcement to Deadwood residents that they need to evacuate. And YOU need to evacuate as soon as you make the announcement," Carnahan says. "The fire is encroaching on the town and we cannot guarantee your safety. Get out while you can."

Harry looks out the studio window, which frames his view of the fire. It's consuming everything. He can see the men working to rescue the houses just down the hillside from his station. Firefighters are furiously working to put out fire in the grass as it advances toward the station. The men also work to prevent it from reaching the lower branches of nearby trees. They use giant hoses to wet the grass and trees not yet on fire and to drench the burning buildings. Harry can just see the water arcing over the nearby houses as the firefighters spray the buildings.

In preparation, Harry has gathered wet towels and placed them at the cracks of the studio doorway and windows. He has filled several thermoses and jugs with water just in case the utilities are shut off.

"Yeah," Harry chuckles a bit. "I can see the men working on buildings below us, right here. But you know, I can't leave the station now. How will folks get the latest, breaking news? How will they know where the fire is? I can relay messages faster than a hundred phone calls. You know, as well as I do, that not every household has a television to rely on. I'll stay on as long as the station can broadcast," he replies. "Keep feeding me what you want me to share with the public."

"Don't be a hero, Harry. You know we can't guarantee your safety if you stay," William Carnahan states. He is talking fast because he needs to get busy directing firefighters.

"You know me, man—always the rebel," Harry responds and gives a shout of laughter. "Besides, this building is just poured concrete and glass. Not much to burn 'cept the wires. If you and your firefighters can keep the wires from burning, I'll stay on the air. Hey! A great idea just popped—how about those firefighters hose down the station after they get that house soaked. Then the fire will go around me."

"Well, you are darned right, Harry. You will soon be surrounded by fire. Get out now! If the fire doesn't get you, the smoke will. I can't save you if you stay!" Carnahan is shouting into the phone.

"If it comes to that, make sure the paper spells my name right," Harry replies unshaken. Clearly aware that the odds are against him, Harry hangs up the phone.

Interrupting 'Mack the Knife', he directs all of us waiting for more information.

"Breaking news, folks. This is Harry Daniels

coming to you live from KDSJ. Those of you living in Deadwood are asked to evacuate. This is the third evacuation notice, so if you live in Deadwood and you haven't gone yet, get gone. Take as few items as possible. You should really be heading out of town right now. There are National Guard and State Patrol directing traffic," he says in as level a voice as he can muster. He doesn't want to panic folks, but knows he needs to create a sense of urgency.

~ ~ ~ ~ ~

Just a short hour later, Harry shares a new warning, as he reports to his listeners, "For those Deadwood residents evacuating, be aware that Highway 14A has been cut off. Please head south toward Highway 85A. I repeat, do not attempt to evacuate using Highway 14A. It is engulfed in flames. Head out of town toward Spearfish or Rapid City. The civic centers will have temporary space for you."

We sit glued to the radio and TV impatiently waiting for the announcement for us to evacuate. Each minute seems like an eternity. The smell of smoke seems stronger than before, and our eyes are beginning to sting. I can feel the fire growing and getting closer.

"I sure hope Jolene got out before the fire crossed Highway 14A. I told her the other route would probably be faster. I hope she changed her mind and went south." Mom worried out loud.

~ ~ ~ ~ ~

Aunt Jolene sees the red horizon through the haze of smoke. She and cousins Debbie, Cathy Jo, and Mike all hurried to leave their home in Deadwood. Stuck in their car, on Highway 14A, the road is packed with cars in both directions. Everyone waits for the fire patrol to direct them. They have been shuttled out of town, but now must double-back because the fire has crossed the road. Ash descends like snow, and Aunt Jolene murmurs a silent prayer.

The trees on the north side of the road up ahead explode with fire. The car shakes with the impact of the blast. It sounds like a battalion of angry wasps are surrounding the car, and burning embers rain down on the traffic sitting on the road. Debbie and Cathy let out screams and Mike shouts, "WOW! That was awesome!"

To escape the firestorm, some of the cars attempt to turn around in the middle of the road. This leads to a bigger road block. The car in front of Aunt Jolene backs up. Bump! It hits her car, then moves forward at a sharp turn and backs up again. It edges forward between two cars going in the opposite direction. Horns honk, honk, honk! Then the car shoots around the line of cars. Traveling along the shoulder of the road, it goes the length of about six cars. Suddenly it slides down the incline, then rolls over once, twice—

smashing bushes on the way down. A small tree breaks and falls as the car comes to a stop in the ditch. It is upside down, with the tree straddling it. Aunt Jolene gasps!

~ ~ ~ ~ ~

Harry continues his broadcast, "Those of you living in Lead are asked to be ready to go. But wait! You are in no immediate danger. It is safer in your homes than on the highways right now. The roads are bumper to bumper and the going is very slow."

Smoke continues to fill the broadcasting room. Harry places more wet towels on the floor in front of the door and along the window sills. Back on the air, he repeats the message before noticing that the station phone lines are flashing. Harry Daniels has enlisted dozens of people as spotters. From forestry personnel and firefighters to neighbors and friends who know he is broadcasting and have pledged to give him live updates. In this way he can more accurately tell listeners how the fire is progressing and what is being done to battle the blaze. Then he pushes the button for a pre-recorded commercial, he coughs and blows his nose.

Harry shares updates, then refills his thermos and another water container from the dwindling water tank. It is now warm water, but even so it will help him stay alive. Harry's voice is getting rough; the increasing smoke causes him to choke and cough often. The thermometer in the radio station reads 100 degrees and he is sweating profusely. Harry takes off his tie and wraps it around his head, front to back, so the sweat will stop running into his eyes. Then he takes off his dress shirt. His T-shirt underneath is fully soaked with sweat.

Everyone listens like our lives depend on it, which I guess they do.

6

Climbing

Mom and Aunt Dolly send us kids outside while they begin fixing supper. They turned off the television as soon as the radio came back on, since they were getting more news about the fire from Harry. Anyway, they didn't want all of us kids sitting around the living room.

"We'll let you all know what's happening. Go out and play a little while longer, while you can," they say.

We march outside and mill around in the yard before heading, once again, to the tall pine at the north edge of our yard. It seems that the tree calls us, or we all naturally gravitate toward it. At any rate, the tree is where we older kids most often gather.

The eighty-foot-tall pine is a test of daring and agility and has come to determine the extent of our bravery. Moxie, mojo, grit, backbone, courage, bravery, pluck, mettle, strength of will, and fortitude all come to the minds of us kids who have braved the tree—and returned fearlessly. Okay, maybe we didn't all do it fear-

The Ponderosa Pine we kids climbed.

Ponderosa Pines: Days of the Deadwood Forest Fire

lessly, but we have conquered fear well enough to do the deed. In addition, we have made a game of finding new words to describe bravery, but they all mean the same thing: we've achieved "Big Kid" status.

I'm proud of the word I found—"pluck," which I discovered when I was looking up a different word for pick or take. I didn't know a word can be a verb AND a noun and that they have different meanings. That was like a secret, and I keep that knowledge in my pocket for future use.

A word can be a verb and a noun. Who knew?

David has finally climbed up five branches, and then down, without help. This is the first time he has climbed the tree and returned successfully. Feeling so proud of himself, he walks around, chest out, smiling at everyone.

Up next is cousin Ronny. He's a tall and skinny eight-year-old with a carrot-topped head, as red as his mom, Aunt Dolly. Ronny gets to the fourth branch and stops. "Okay. Okay. This is too prickly. I'm gettin' pitched," he grumbles. "Coming down!"

"You big wuss," Lenny says, when Ronny is on the ground. He and Ronny are like differently colored twins. Lenny, like Ronny is also as skinny as a beanpole. Both boys are usually skinned up and bruised in a variety of places. Same but different, Lenny has jet-black hair instead of red and is tanned to a rich nut brown from the summer past. He will hang on to his tan through at least December. Ronny is pink-skinned as a newborn piglet, just like many other red-heads, and his mom likes to say that "he's freckled to within an inch of his life." Both boys have dark brown eyes and they unconsciously match each other's swaggering walk and talk. The competition between them is constant and fierce.

"I'm goin' up to the eighth branch this time!" Lenny boasts. When he gets to the called branch, he decides to go one higher. Then one higher yet. "I think I got the gold. Ten branches! This is higher'n any of you even climbed. I win!" he brags, as he begins the descent back down.

"Y'all know I climbed to the top already. That's fifteen branches," twelve-year-old Betty says quietly.

"Hey. . . I really smelled the fire from up there," Lenny says, almost to himself as he climbs back down. He jumps from the last branch and claps his hands together when he is back on terra firma. Then, with hands on his hips, he struts around the yard like a crowing rooster.

"Well . . . you gonna' defend your record, or let him have his swagger?" Betty asks quietly turning to me.

"I suppose I have to," I say, and reluctantly walk over and slowly begin to climb the tall pine. I have already proven my mettle, but need to reaffirm my place as a big kid each time a new challenge is delivered. Climbing the tree takes bravery, and I have to screw up my courage to even begin. Ronny is right, the tree is prickly and the pine pitch sticks on my clothing like molasses. The orange-brown bark of the tree trunk has thin irregular plates or scales that remind me of jigsaw puzzle pieces. Pine pitch oozes, but finding dry spots to hold onto can be done. The branches have clumps of long pine needles that are farther out on the branch, leaving a narrow section empty enough for a thin someone to climb up. Even so, I look to see where the needles are before grabbing each branch. This tree's sharp, dried-out needles are ready to fall off at a touch. They readily stick to my clothes and hair.

Once I begin, the fear seems to lessen. Easily, I reach the eighth branch, then the ninth. The smell of pine is strong within the tree's branches, and it feels cooler than out in the evening air. It is almost like air conditioning. I stop climbing and breathe deeply. The clean pine scent is so strong that it clears my stuffy nose. Once I ascend the tree, I love being on the branches. I'm alone. The sounds below are muted and distant. They seem more remote the higher I climb. There is a breeze that makes the tree sway. As I go higher, the tree trunk narrows and the sway feels more dramatic. I like it better when there is no wind—no sway in the tree.

It is breathtaking to be so high. Drawing in a breath through pursed lips, I take in air like a hummingbird sips nectar—greedily and delicately at the same time. The entire town is visible through the tree limbs.

Lead is a town whose main street is situated

neatly in the valley, with homes stacked into the terraced hillsides on either side. Looking north, I can see several of the stepped homes and yards directly below ours. The houses climbing the mountain on the other side mirror what I see below.

Wow, I didn't know Hansen's had a new Buick. Looks like they're gettin' ready to leave town, too.

Turning to look northeast, I see a wide column of smoke dancing on the mountainside. Tips of flames shoot up at the edges of the smoke column. The smell of burning wood is strong. A forest fire has a completely different smell than that of houses or meadows, and this smell is definitely trees.

The fire! It looks alive. And it looks hungry. It is really eating up the forest! It's strange to see it burning. It looks surprisingly close—so much closer than I thought. I wonder how Dad and Uncle Roger are? It is unbelievable to see the fire from up here rather than on the ground.

My worry is quickly lost as Lenny yells up at me. "Well, are you gonna' just sit there, or are you goin' higher?"

"Yeah. You goin' higher?" Richie repeats the catcall. He always repeats everything the older boys say.

"Yeah. Yeah. I was just admiring the view up here," I respond.

I am standing on the eighth branch, holding the ninth, so two more to go. Nine. Ten. Okay, one more to make it real.

I place my feet on the ninth and tenth branches and reach up, strategizing as I climb.

"I'm standin' on eleven," I call down to the others.

"No, you're not. That looks like the tenth branch to me," Lenny yells up.

"Oh, how would you know? You ain't up here!" I shout back to him.

I'll go one more just to show you, Lenny!

Now the wind sends a strong gust to sway the tree, and me along with it. I clutch the main trunk as the feeling of vertigo hits me. My heart pounds in my ears. I gasp, suck in breath and hold it there with my eyes squeezed tightly shut. The large tree trunk has narrowed considerably and, with my arms, I easily hug all the way around it as pine pitch smears my cheek and sticks in my hair.

It seems like a year passes with me in the darkness of eyes-closed fear. The wind has slowed to a gentle blowing. Finally, I open my eyes and can hear the world again.

"Annette . . . Annette, are you OK?" Betty calls up. "You aren't stuck, are ya?"

"Well . . . Well . . . I am a little," I say softly. The wind sways the tree again bringing with it a definite smell of burning pine, and I say in a wavery voice, "Yes. Yes! I'm stuck." I clutch the tree a little tighter. More pitch and needles settle onto my face and into my hair.

"Annette, you can do it . . . Come on down . . .

You did it before," Betty calls.

Pretty soon five or six voices are calling up to me. "You can do it. Come on down!"

"Put your left foot on the next lower branch. Now let go of the tree trunk and just put your hand on the branch," Betty says. And so, siblings and cousins—but mostly Betty—talk me down, limb by limb, until I'm out of the tree.

"You made it, and you went higher than Lenny," Betty says to me as I put my feet on solid ground.

"Buuuuuttt . . . You don't win 'cause you got coached down," Lenny interjects. "So, I still got the gold, 'cept for Betty." He smiles and struts around the yard with his hands on his hips, then back to us girls.

"My ten branches are still gold! And I beat YOU!" He smiles a proud smile and sticks his tongue out at me.

"You big baby," Ronny says, leaning toward me.

"Big baby," Richie repeats.

"Hey!" David says. "It's scary up there, especially when the wind blows and shakes the tree."

"Oh, blubber baby, David!" Richie says, a little louder.

"You take that back!" David says. And then the two boys are wrestling around on the ground.

I lower my head, embarrassed.

I did go higher than Lenny. But it was true, I got scared and had to be talked down. I'm such a coward. When will I be brave enough not to be so scared of climbing down?

They're right, I am a big baby! The boys are younger than me, yet they climb up the tree without worrying. I should be able to do this!

"Suppertime! Come on in and wash up," Mom calls from the house.

"Hey! You two! Stop wrestling in the dirt. Those are your brand-new school clothes you are getting all dirty. What is the matter with you? Can't you keep anything new for even a short time?" Mom is yelling at David and Richie who are still wrestling. She takes a single step out the front door, which is a sign she's gonna give someone a spank.

The boys stop wrestling and stand up, looking at Mom. "Uh, okay, Mom," says David. "I'm sorry." He stuffs his fists into his pants pockets and starts walking toward the house.

"Okay, Auntie Anne," Richie says. "I'm sorry, too." He also stuffs his fists into his pants pockets. Pretty soon both boys are racing in a fast walk to the house, still competing.

Mom looks at them and shakes her head as they skim by her in the doorway.

"Wash up those dirty hands and faces!" she calls to their backs.

We all head for the house, with us older kids rounding up the younger ones and making sure they get into the bathroom to wash hands for supper.

I help Valerie wash up, then use the soap to scrub my own face and neck. It takes three or four "wash, scrub, rinse" cycles to get most of the pitch off, and there are angry red marks every place I've been successful. From the looks of my hair, it will be hard to get a brush or comb through it and I decide to work on it tonight, right after supper.

"Annette! What is that all over your clothes and in your hair? OH MY GOODNESS! How many times have I told you kids not to climb that tree? Just look at you! Now, I'll have a dickens-of-a-time getting that pine pitch out of your clothing. I swear! You kids just keep inventing ways for me to do more work!" Mom scolds.

I am ashamed. I know Mom is right and I am one of the older kids, so I should know better. At least that's what Mom always says. "You should know better." I wonder when I will "know better." I try really hard to keep the single tear from rolling down my cheek. And I almost succeed.

7

Supper Time

During our supper, talk is all about the fire and we kids want an update. Lenny is sharing a chair with Ronny as they shovel food into their mouths, bite for bite. The five little kids are lined up on the bench and send their gaze from speaker to speaker. Doreen and I bookend the bench to keep the other five in check.

"Hey, Mom, what about the fire?" Lenny asks.

"Yeah, what about the fire? Where is it now? We can see the smoke and flames," David says. He and Richie share a chair, like Lenny and Ronny, but they struggle more with their space. And one or the other of them is on the floor several times during each meal.

"Yeah, we seen smoke and flames," repeats Richie. He and David look at each other to affirm what was said. They turn simultaneously to look at Mom who is putting food onto the high chair tray for baby Mark. Mark happily gurgles and lifts his baby fork into the air.

He has no clue! Is that a bad thing or is it somehow better?

"We can smell the smoke, too," Doreen adds.

"Yeah. I could even smell the smoke in the tree," I say. Mom gives me a look.

"AND, the smell of burnt-up is getting stronger," Lenny says.

"Mom, you know, we could go now. We're all packed and it's still light out. Let's go while we can see where we're goin'," Ronny says to Aunt Dolly.

"Yeah, Mom, let's get outa' town," Lenny says.

"Let's get outa' town," Richie repeats.

"We know there is a forest fire nearby. Actually, we know parts of Deadwood have burned and the fire is northeast of the town, but that's pretty much all we know," Mom says.

"Oh, and Highway 14A is blocked off. But we wouldn't take that road anyway. Plus, the roads are full, bumper to bumper, actually. We should wait until there are fewer cars on the roads because we can't get out in any kind of hurry anyway," Aunt Dolly adds.

"Are we vac-watin?" Valerie asks. Her little face is smudged despite a recent wash. Her light blonde hair is tangled and dirty. I'm pretty sure I'll be assigned to give her a bath, just by looking at her hair.

"That is EEE-vac-YOU-ATE-ing." Doreen says "evacuating" with as much emphasis as she can. Then she looks smugly around the table at us other kids because she knows about this big word.

"No, not yet. We need to wait for them to tell us which way to go, to get out of town," Mom responds. "But we have the car almost packed and ready, so we can just hop in and leave as soon as they tell us to."

"Why don't they tell us to 'vac - YOU - at?" asks Stevie.

"Yeah!" repeats Richie, "Why don't they tell us to git outa' town?"

"Let's git while the gittin's good!" David says, and pounds his fist into his other hand.

"Well, my git up and go, got up an went! Now, I'm left with the likes of you all," Mom says with a slow smile. She looks at Aunt Dolly who smiles as well.

Aunt Dolly gets up and goes to the radio to turn it up when she hears the voice of Joe Schmitline who is saying, "The firefighters from the forest service have rushed to fight the blaze as fire managers decide how best to organize the fight. They have been expecting a forest fire for quite some time. Conditions have been ripe for it. Yet, none of us wanted such a blaze.

"The miners from the Homestake Gold Mine have been called to join the forest rangers and firefighters to battle the blaze.[9] The men are all wearing denim jeans, long sleeved shirts, and leather boots—the uniform for their work in the mine. They'll keep their miner helmets and gloves to protect themselves from the intense heat they will encounter. Each man brought his pick ax or shovel and filled his thermos with water. Those filled thermoses may well save a man's life at some point in the next few hours.

"There are now over 3,600 volunteers, foresters and firefighters working to put out this fire. Homes and businesses in Deadwood are burning, and it looks like a battle zone.[10] Deadwood Gulch is thick with low-hanging, dense smoke making eyes sting and lungs ache. Bulldozers, water tankers, trucks, and other heavy equipment are speeding through Deadwood toward the fire.

"Pastors of churches, off duty police, doctors, nurses and their spouses, professional men and school girls will be working in shifts to feed the firefighters and provide a spot for the men to rest. These volunteers are camped out at the Franklin Hotel on Main Street in downtown Deadwood, which has become the headquarters for the rescue operation."[11]

He pauses to cough and clear his throat before signing off, leaving us all wondering why he didn't tell us to get out, why he didn't tell us to get out right now!

"This is Joe Schmitline, "the Voice of the News," here in the Black Hills, signing off from KDSJ." Harry Daniels comes back on and plays a commercial, then another song.

"Mom! I'm scared. We should go 'afore the fire gets us," Becky says. She goes over and crawls on Aunt Dolly's lap.

"Yeah. I'm a'scared, too," says Valerie, and she goes over and stands by Mom, who puts a comforting arm around her. I feel pretty scared myself. As I look around the table, I see that all the boys have large round eyes. My sister Betty is fidgeting with her blouse buttons, which is a sure sign she's scared, too. My teeth clench and I look at Mom to see what she will say.

"We can hang on a little while longer. Let's just be patient," Mom says in an "everybody calm down" manner. She puts her arm more snuggly around Valerie and hugs her more tightly. Charlie slips off the bench and comes over. Mom gives him a hug, too.

"Hey, supper's on the table. Let's eat now," Aunt Dolly says, like it is a big surprise and we all don't already have food on our plates. We all turn our attention to eating. The boys seem to inhale their food, but I've lost my appetite.

~ ~ ~ ~ ~

Meanwhile, the fire has intensified as it moves up the mountain. More wind is blowing. More and more trees are burning. More and more volunteers and equipment are needed to stop this fire. Dad and Uncle Roger, along with other miners, are fighting with as much strength as they can. Roger is with a crew along that same Highway 14A where his wife is stuck in traffic. The crew begins by cutting trees and bull-dozing them into a ridge close up to the forest and away from the road. They work fast, sweating and panting to get the forest cleared before the fire reaches them. The air is so hot and full of ash that Roger has wet his large handkerchief and tied it like a mask over his nose and mouth. Even while wearing his safety glasses, Roger's eyes sting and tear up. As they work, they see the fire coming closer and closer. Roger has brought his pick axe and a shovel, and he hands the axe to another volunteer. Some folks are wearing baseball caps and others like Roger, wear helmets. The going is slow because the forest is dense and firefighters must move up and down steep inclines to do their work. Like other men, Roger is silently thinking of his family and his home in Deadwood. He feels his heart beating in his throat, but knows he cannot wimp out no matter how he feels. He keeps working despite his growing fear and concern for his family. As Roger fights the forest to clear the way, he feels the fire is so much bigger, more immediate than when they practiced. He knows what to do, but drills didn't emphasize the intense heat, the dense smoke and ash, and how hard it would be to breathe.

The crew has been clearing the forest for about three hours as the smoke gets even more dense and the fire races closer. Someone yells "Timber!" and a great pine tree keels over! Roger looks up and sees the tree falling. It looms larger and larger as it falls. He begins to run, but a branch from a smaller tree snags his trousers and he trips. As Roger stumbles, the tree crashes down on top of him.

8

Chokecherries!

After supper, Mom and Aunt Dolly decide to keep us kids all together until bedtime so they can both hear the news at the same time if we get the evacuation call. They typically lean on one another, but this has us all wanting to stay close to support each other.

We have heard once again the evacuation notice for Deadwood and wonder when the announcement for us to go will be aired. Now that the miners have been called to the fire, we are all fretting about Uncle Roger and Dad.

Our station wagon is packed with apples, loaves of bread, peanut butter, two canned hams, carrot sticks, cherry tomatoes, an emergency first aid kit, one change of clothing for everyone, blankets, diapers, and several jugs of water. We wait for the call to evacuate Lead, knowing that a lot of people in town have already left. The waiting is worse than going. The urge to leave, now that we are ready, feels immediate.

Why wait? Let's just go. But, go where?

Now that supper is over, some of the younger

kids go outside to play tag while us older kids do homework. There is no television during school nights, but Mom still has the radio on low and is listening to 'Lipstick on Your Collar' by Connie Francis.

I am absentmindedly humming along with the tune. I just love Connie Francis. But my absolute favorite singer is Miss Patsy Cline. I hope one of Patsy's songs will come on next. Doreen looks at me and we mouth the words to "Lipstick on Your Collar," not doing our reading at all. We smile at each other as the song ends, then return to our homework.

Betty concentrates so deeply, her sandy-blonde head bent over her new science book, that she fails to hear the radio, or anything anyone is saying.

Lenny, David, Ronny, and Richie are sitting at the table with books open, but they haven't even begun the assigned homework. "I don't know how they expect us to do homework when the younger kids get to play all the time," Lenny complains.

"Yeah, they should have to work, too," David says, even though he has finished his schoolwork and has his book open to support the rest of us—and because Mom said so.

Both Ronny and Richie nod in agreement. They can't understand why they got homework on the first day of school, anyway. None of us can. Plus, no one can sit still long enough to concentrate on schoolwork because the urge to leave is making us all jumpy and distracted.

"Okay, okay, you kids. Get busy. You spend more time complaining about homework than it would take to just get it done," Mom says, and I think she might be right.

I quickly look at my assignment again and re-read the three assigned pages of my science book. I haven't kept a bit of the information I read the first time. I'm a fast reader. I actually love to read, just not the textbooks they give us. Most of us kids are good readers. Both Mom and Dad read all the time. We older kids check out library books every week. Even three-year-old Chuck wants to read a book. Yup, we are a reading family. Almost any Sunday afternoon, you will find several of us, if not the whole family, reading something.

Next, I pull the sheet of math problems out and begin by writing my name at the top. Math does not come as easily as reading, so I try to settle my mind and focus on the problems on the page. The numbers swim up and down, then begin to dance. It's useless. I trace the letters of my name again and decide to put today's date at the top, as well.

Meanwhile, the younger kids, have tired of their running game. They begin picking the chokecherries from the very lowest branches of the tree. I see them through the kitchen window above the sink. A couple kids pick cherries off the ground and gather them in their hands or slip them into pockets.

The large, overgrown chokecherry tree has branches hanging over the back fence like grapevines.

The limbs are loaded and the cherries taste just fine—tart with a touch of sweetness. Each chokecherry has a small, hard stone and us kids think that is what the "choke" is all about with these small fruits. The kids pull on the overhanging branches to get more of the fruit.

"Hey! You kids! Get away from my tree! You varmints!" yells the owner of said tree. "Get away, I say!" He charges the fence with a large broom raised above his head.

The children scatter, screaming and running to the front door of the house, which is around the corner, down the length of the house to the opposite side. They are carrying handfuls of chokecherries as they run.

"Mom! Mom! Mr. Leroy yelled at us! He shook his broom at us!" Stevie gasps, out of breath from running, his five-year-old body lean and muscular. Dark hair shades his brown eyes and his face is flushed from the quick getaway. The purple stains around his mouth and on his chin are evidence of the number of chokecherries he has already eaten.

Right on his heels, Becky repeats every word. "Mr. Leroy yelled at us! He shook his broom!" Her strawberry blonde hair dances as she hops up and down while repeating the tale.

"Yes. He DID! Shh. . sh. . . shook his broom at us! He was gonna'. . . he . . . he might hit us!" Valerie shouts, stuttering a little in her haste. She has large brown eyes, light brown hair to match, and has the shrillest scream of anyone we know. She is genuinely frightened of the neighbor and quakes a little as she stands with a handful of fruit in front of Mom.

"Me, too. Me, too," says Charlie. His brown eyes have a smile instead of a scared look as he lifts his three-year-old hands to the counter and dumps the reward. He thinks the whole thing is a game. He loved the running and, after handing his fruit to Mom, he does a run around the table before Aunt Dolly grabs him to stop the running.

Ralphie pulls two chokecherries from his pockets and pushes one into Mom's waiting hands, then puts the other one into his mouth. The kids all stand looking up at Mom with their cherry-stained faces, waiting for her to make everything all right again.

Baby Mark toddles over to them as soon as he sees the chokecherries. He knows they are tasty and is hoping for a treat. His ash blond hair falls into his almond shaped, hazel eyes. His chubby, baby body is just beginning to stretch out as he grows. His baby arms cannot reach the counter, but he is an efficient climber, so we all keep an eye out for how and where he might climb.

"How many times have I told you NOT to put those chokecherries in your pockets?" Mom says as she gathers the fruit into a bowl. "I can never get the stains out. Your clothes will be ruined."

"But, Mom," Stevie looks at her beseechingly, "what about Mr. Leroy?".

"I'll ask your father to speak to him later," Mom replies. "It's time for you all to get ready for bed, anyway." She picks up baby Mark and places him securely on one hip as she continues putting the chokecherries into the bowl. She rinses a cherry, bites the pit out and pops the fruit into Mark's mouth.

"Mmmmm!" he says and smiles at her. Mom smiles back and gives him a squeeze. Then she looks at Aunt Dolly and they both smile a resigned smile, knowing wash day will have more challenge with those stubborn stains.

David, Lenny, Ronny, and Richie have overheard the commotion and the conversation. They each grab a bowl from the cupboard and sidle out the door. Stealth is their name as they ease around the corner of the house, crouching low, and sneak along the northern side. They peek around the northwest corner of the house, gaze across the garden and around to the tree. Mr. Leroy is standing there looking angrily at our house. He shakes his broom again at no one in particular.

"Darned, varmint kids!" he yells one last time, then turns and stomps back to his house. Through the kitchen window, I watch him retreat and I smile, because I know exactly what the boys are up to. They wait a minute or two—not long enough really. Moving quiet and low, they reach the tree limbs hanging like so many Christmas stockings, full of sweet, sweet treasure. Since the big boys are taller than the little kids, they can reach higher. They each take a branch and quickly fill their bowls with chokecherries, smiling widely at each other. They got the goods! They eat as many as they gather into their bowls.

"Uh-huh, mmm, uh-huh, mmm," mumbles Richie as he munches chokecherries.

"Mmmm. Mmmm. Mmmm," replies David. He shoots Richie a smile and they exchange a thumbs-up sign, then continue filling their bowls.

Lenny finishes a cherry then spits the stone in a high arc toward the south end of the yard. Ronny does the same. His stone lands a few feet short of Lenny's so they each spit another stone trying to outdo each other, making a short game of who can spit seeds the farthest.

"You know, I think the air is really full of smoke," Ronny says in a real low voice.

"That's prob'ly right. Yeah. The air does feel thick, doesn't it? I wonder how close the fire is," Lenny says, and he wonders when we will go. His black hair hangs over his ears and eyebrows and he gives his head a shake to send the unwanted locks away from his eyes.

"Let's get our moms to leave soon! Just get in the car and go. Right now!" he says to Ronny who is gathering berries and is thinking virtually the same thing. "Yes, Let's leave soon. Let's just get in the car and go!"

The boys finish filling their bowls with the cherries, popping as many in their mouths as into the bowls and spitting the seeds. Soon they sneak back along the north side of the house and in the front door. Only as they enter the kitchen do they whoop and congratulate each other for their prowess and cunning.

"Hey, Auntie Anne, I jus' happen 'ta find these layin' 'round the backyard 'n thought you could do sompin' wit' 'em," Ronny drawls, with his smile as wide as a Sunday afternoon, and he laughs a "we showed him" laugh.

"Yeah, we jus' found these layin' 'round," Lenny laughs too, as he hands his bowl to Mom.

"Yeah! We all did. Find 'em, I mean," Richie chimes in. His seven-year-old hands grasp the bowl still. He would like to eat all the fruit in his bowl instead of turning it over to Mom. He is not as tall and skinny as his brother or cousin. His body is short and stocky. His hair is not the dynamic red of his brother, but a sandy color that his mom and sisters call "dishwater blonde," making it seem less desirable than other hair colors, but it suits him well. Mom says his sandy-blonde hair makes him seem like a California surfer.

"OH! You boys!" Mom says. She takes each offered bowl and places them near the sink to rinse later. "Here you are making more work for me!" she says and shakes her head. "I probably have enough for jelly, now," she smiles, then turns to face them. "But you boys know it is NOT correct, nor Christian to lie. You DID NOT find these lying around on the ground," Mom corrects them, even though she is still smiling.

Both David and Richie bow their heads and

mumble, "Sorry."

Lenny and Ronny just nod their heads. They are not sorry in the least.

"Hey, Mom! We smelled lots of smoke out there when we were pickin', I mean findin'. . . okay, so we picked those chokecherries. But we smelled a lot of smoke, too," David says, and his troubled look transfers to Mom instantly. He is a bit stockier than Lenny, his older brother, so David and Richie seem like twins. They are the same age and in the same class at school. David's hair is dark brown, almost black, so the teacher tells them apart by their hair color. David and Richie are fast friends who wrestle, wrangle, and wring-out as much trouble and fun as they can muster. They are usually following the bigger boys around, but don't much mind being second. When the play gets too tough, they strike out on their own and leave their big brothers to watch the younger kids. Sometimes second-in-command has its advantages.

"And Mom, you know they ARE in our yard, so it's fair game," Lenny defends their actions.

"Well, it's still not right to lie, no matter what," she scolds, a bit more sternly this time. "And besides, you guys are supposed to be doing your homework. Get back to it. Right now—but, wash your hands first. They are probably purple with juice." When the boys come back from the bathroom, Mom points to the table until they all trudge back and sit down again.

"But, Mom, what about the smoke? When are

we gonna' go?" David asks, and we all look at Mom anxiously.

"Yeah, Mom, we should just get gone," Lenny says.

"Get gone!" Richie repeats.

9

The News

Mom puts her hand to her chin and says, "More smoke? Hmm. OK, let's see if the television has anything more to say about where the fire is headed. I haven't heard a word from the radio about Lead evacuating," she mumbles, sounding a little disappointed that her favorite station has not informed her in time.

"Mom, is Dad fightin' on the fire?" Stevie asks. The urge to flee is building in his small body so that he feels like a tightly coiled spring. He can't help running around the table now and again.

"Yes, honey. He and Uncle Roger were called out of the mine with all the other men to help fight the fire," she replies. "And I suppose it's bound to be smoky here as the wind sends it all our way. It's probably hazy all over the Black Hills by now. Go get a drink of water when your throat feels too scratchy."

Mom turns on the television to Channel 3, KO-TA-TV, and we girls stop doing homework. Everyone gathers around the television. There is a newscaster announcing "Late Breaking News!" He is reporting that the fire now has Deadwood surrounded on three sides. Highways 14A and 85A going north are both cut off from travel. They are no longer exit routes. More volunteers are needed to fight the fire. The mayor has asked the National Guard from Ellsworth Air Force base to join the effort.

"The miners from the Homestake Gold Mine have been called to join the forest rangers and firefighters to battle the blaze. We have forest rangers, highway patrolmen, the National Guardsmen, forest firefighters from other states, and a large number of citizen volunteers all working together to put out this blaze," the announcer says.

"Now, over to Glenda Watkins in Deadwood." The screen moves from the studio to downtown Deadwood.

"Mom, we heard this before," Doreen says. "How come they are saying the same thing all over again?"

"Well, some folks might not have heard, and the newscasters repeat things when there isn't so much new news to tell," Aunt Dolly explains. "Or they repeat news to remind us of what we already heard, so when they add new information, we will understand."

"Flames lap along Deadwood city limits like waves of an incoming tide. The streets are dense with low hanging smoke that makes visibility on the east side of Deadwood less than half a city block and breathing almost impossible," says Glenda, standing in front of the Franklin Hotel with a hankie up to her mouth.

"The men who are working to put out the blazing commercial buildings have been joined by other firefighting teams who will help put out the house fires. Deadwood businesses are all closed tonight during this terrible, terrible disaster. Our brave firefighters have also turned their hoses on nearby homes to wet them down, in a hopeful attempt to save the surrounding buildings. As soon as the fire consumes one building it begins to devour another," she sounds like she's calling a football game. Now the television shows footage of the fire on the roads and the hillsides and of buildings lit up with flames.

Glenda continues in an even more dramatic voice. "The fire is a wild thing. It races along the treetops crowning the trees like a tiara. Nothing can withstand the terrific heat it produces as it gobbles up air and wood. In several spots, the wind blows firebrands away, shooting them like fireballs that arc to not-yet-burning trees or brush, which burst into flames. In this way the fire has multiplied and spread until the whole mountaintop is raw and blazing," she looks intently into the camera with a serious face. Then, she smiles and turns to the man standing beside her.

"I'm here at the command post with Sheriff McGrath who is in charge of fighting this terrible blaze." She adds, "Sherriff McGrath, thank you for taking your precious time to talk with me and inform our viewers. Can you give us an update?"

Sherriff McGrath looks intently at Glenda, then begins. "Forty houses in Deadwood have burned to the ground! Evacuation of the hospital in Deadwood has just finished. Patients have been moved to the Homestake Hospital in Lead. Evacuees are streaming out of Deadwood in all directions, despite the warnings," he says in a scolding voice, then continues, "Folks, you will find that several highways going north and east are cut off as flames burn the forest on either side of the roads. Please do NOT go this way. Traveling north or east leads to traffic congestion as people go out, then have to turn around and come back into town to leave on another highway. The streets are congested with traffic," he concludes, then moves quickly off screen.

Aunt Dolly enters with Ralphie at that moment, and we are now all in the living room, looking at the television. Thirteen children and two women who all feel a growing sense of panic, who all feel the need to flee—and flee fast.

"Pretty soon, we won't have a way to leave, anymore," I overhear Aunt Dolly whisper to Mom. They exchange worried looks.

"Let's not get the kids riled up any more than they already are," Mom whispers, and starts putting the younger kids to bed. We older ones are allowed to stay up a while longer watching television, reading, or playing cards. Some of us have to go back and finish our homework. I spend another fifteen minutes on math, then just give it up. I close up my books, notebooks, and folders, then put them back into my school pack. Mom and Aunt Dolly talk in low tones about whether to go or stay. I can see the indecision as plain as day, on their faces.

"Mom, why are you putting us to bed? Shouldn't we just leave instead of going to sleep? What if they call us to evacuate and we are all asleep?" I ask.

I can't stand to stay. I feel like jumping out of my skin. I should just go sit in the car until it's time to go. I wonder how long it would take to walk out of here, or run? How long to just run away?

"Let's go. Let's just go," I say again.

"Honey, we can't just leave until we know where to go and which highway is clear. Besides, they will surely get the fire under control and we won't have to leave at all," Mom says in a way that is supposed to calm me. But she doesn't sound convincing at all.

The news comes on again and Lenny shouts, pointing at the television. "Hey, look! It's Uncle Roger!"

"No. It can't be him. You don't know that's him," Betty says and she moves closer to the television set.

"I think you're right, Lenny. That is Roger," Mom says as if dazed.

"Wow! I have never seen someone I know on TV, ever before," David says. "And he's someone I'm related to!"

"Me too, neither—seen Uncle Roger on TV," says Richie.

"I know," whispers Becky, in awe as well. Five-year-old Becky has just put on her pajamas and has had her long strawberry blonde hair brushed. She hasn't lost what her mother calls her "baby fat," and is a dumpling of a child. Her disposition is as sweet as she looks and everybody loves her. She makes friends easily and kindergarten will be fun for her. Stevie will be in the same grade, but they are not in the same class. She walks over to the couch and climbs onto her brother, Ronny's lap. He accepts her without a word. Everyone is mesmerized by the television.

The newscaster is standing alongside some firefighters who are sitting on the running edge of a fire truck drinking water from thermoses.

"Two National Guardsmen were injured when the fire overtook their bulldozer. And we have another man who was injured by a falling tree."

The men each have white bandages wrapped around heads or limbs. Uncle Roger is lying on a stretcher.[12] The reporter asks Roger his name and he groans, then states his name in a low, gravelly voice as he is moved toward the ambulance. The newscaster reports that the fire is not yet contained, the men are exhausted, and the forest rangers are calling for more volunteers to help fight the fire. The National Guard has joined with helicopters that are dropping a slurry called bentonite on the hot spots.[13] The television shows the men hoisting Uncle Roger into an ambulance and leaving, sirens blaring.

"I didn't catch that. Did he say he was Roger?"

Aunt Dolly asks.

"Yes. That was him. OUR UNCLE!" David says.

"OUR UNCLE," repeats Richie.

"And your brother!" Ronny shouts. "Mom, your brother was on TV!"

"Shame on that reporter for pushing the mic into his face. Roger looks exhausted and in so much pain!" Mom says. "Yes. I'm pretty sure he said, 'Roger Stabnow'."

"I wish it was Dad on TV instead of Uncle Roger. Then we would be able to see him and know he is all right," I say.

I am a little bit ashamed that I want to see Dad more than Uncle Roger. But I am more scared for Dad. I wonder where he is and how he is doing.

"Yes. It would be great if they were both on TV," Betty says to soften what I've said, even though I'm sure she feels the exact same way. We all search the televised crowd for Dad's black hair and dark eyes, but no one finds him.

Aunt Dolly and Mom have tears in their eyes and move toward each other. They hug and wipe their hands across their eyes.

"He'll be fine," Mom whispers to Aunt Dolly. "Just fine. You'll see."

Dolly nods her head while Mom pats her on the back.

Finally, the television is back to regular programming, and the little kids are all put to bed.

"We'll get you up if they tell us to evacuate," Aunt Dolly assures them.

"Mom, I'm just not sleepy. I wonder what Dad is doing now. How is he? I wonder if we are going to evacuate or if they will get the fire put out. How bad is Uncle Roger hurt? Won't Dad get too tired? Where will he sleep? Where will we go if we leave? How will we get past the fire? Is there a road going south that isn't on fire? How will we all fit into our car? Will the little kids just wear their pajamas? How will Dad find us if we leave?" I say in one long breath.

"I want to stay up awhile, too," Betty says.

"Hush, now. There are so many questions I can't answer tonight. It's been such a long day. I'm exhausted! Shush, or go to bed," Mom says.

"But, can I stay up a while longer? I'm not sleepy at all," I plead. I'm so jumpy I feel like I would not even be able to stay in the bed. Mom nods slightly while she hands a magazine to me, then lights a cigarette and sits down at the table with Aunt Dolly.

"Read something or go to bed," she says.

Mom and Aunt Dolly talk in subdued voices about the cost of the fire to their families, especially if they have to evacuate or lose the house. Mom takes out her purse and counts the money she has. "I think we have enough for a full tank of gas and a little more," she says.

"Well, I think I'm good for about five dollars. No. No, here, I have seven," Aunt Dolly says as she rifles through her purse. She counts out the bills and lays them on the table.

They turn the radio down low and sit near enough to hear if another news announcement breaks into regular programming.

After a while, Betty gets up quietly and goes up the stairs to bed, but I cannot make that move yet.

Mom and Aunt Dolly discuss what else they might need to bring along and what they will have to leave, feeling sad already for the loss of precious possessions. Mom gets up and looks for a photo album to put in the car. Their talk blurs in my ears and mutes to a distant murmur as I turn the pages of the magazine I am not seeing. Finally, I curl up on the couch and doze until Mom sends me upstairs to bed.

10

Smoke Gets in Your Eyes

The night has come and Aunt Jolene is still stuck in traffic. The gas gauge reads at the half-way mark. She worries if it will last. She has been inching forward for two hours and finally sees the firetruck that blocks the road ahead. There are several firemen directing traffic as one car after another slowly turns around and heads back in the opposite direction.

The trees are colored a vibrant orange because they are on fire. There's so much debris in the air that Aunt Jolene has to use the windshield wipers to clean the windshield. It is hotter than ever—and she and the children are having coughing fits. Their eyes stream with tears and the girls are crying.

"I know, sweeties. I know this is hard. But look! We've turned around so we'll be able to get out of the fire soon." Aunt Jolene says, trying to calm her children.

"But, Mom!" says Mike, "We won't be able to go around that tree!"

Just as Mike says that, Jolene hears the noise

and sees a large burning tree crash on the road, only two cars ahead of them. She tries to back up, as does the car in front of her. The car the tree has fallen on is crushed and bursts into flames. She can hear people screaming and a great whooshing sound as the car explodes.

"OH!" Aunt Jolene says, and she covers her eyes. The kids are immediately in the front seat hugging their mother, and they all stay that way until the firefighter knocks on the driver's side window.

~ ~ ~ ~ ~

Listeners, including Mom and Aunt Dolly, hang on every word Harry Daniels says. He's working the phones, pulling and re-shelving records, slipping in commercials, choking and coughing as smoke and heat builds inside his broadcasting room. Sweating profusely and panting, Harry continues to report updates about the fire, even though the smoke in the station makes his eyes sting and water. His engineer has left and Harry is the only person in the building, with a current inside temperature of 102 degrees. The air conditioning has quit. All the windows and doors are closed to prevent additional smoke coming in, and his fan is running intermittently—running and quitting, running and quitting. When it is on, it ineffectively moves the hot air around, but the smoke thins a little. When it is off, the sweat pours down his forehead. The tie tied around his forehead is soaked enough to begin letting the sweat run down his face. He coughs and squints into the control board. He continually sips water from a metal thermos. Harry sees the blinking light on his phone and picks it up.

"KDSJ," Harry says.

"This is Sheriff McGrath letting you know that Highway 385, leading to Custer, Hill City, and Hot Springs has been cut off.[14] Please route folks south through Lead on Highway 85A toward Spearfish."

"Okay, Sheriff," Harry replies with a scared sadness in his voice. "Are you going to give the order to evacuate Lead?"

"No. Not yet. There are too many people on the roads right now. It's like a parking lot out there. Folks just don't follow directions!" He takes a breath and says, "I'm sorry for that last comment."

"I want to give those folks a chance to get out before I put more people on the roads," the sheriff replies. "Southbound 85A is secure enough that we should be able to send them that way when the time comes."

"How goes the fire fighting elsewhere?" Harry asks.

"It's slow and glow," the sheriff says, with a humorless laugh. "We need more help, even with the volunteers coming in as quickly as they are. The Air Force is sending more folks and the air tankers are doing some good. If the winds die down, we'll have a chance." Harry cannot see the man rub his face, but knows the sound of desperation and can relate.

"How are you doing in that station?" the sheriff asks.

"I'm hot as hades, but I'll be okay as long as I don't run out of water. The surrounding area is pretty much burned out, but the smoke is intense. I'd sure like the wind to change direction. The station isn't burning and we are still on the air," Harry replies.

"There's still time for you to get yourself to a safer place. I can send a squad car to get you." the sheriff says.

"Nah. I'm gonna' wait this out," Harry replies.

They chat another minute about the conditions and then, just before hanging up, the sheriff says, "Just pray to God that we get this beast under control before 85A is engulfed, too!"

Harry goes back on the air. "Deadwood is burning," he begins, his voice serious and low. "This is Harry Daniels reporting from KDSJ. The sheriff wants me to find higher ground, but I'm pledged to stay and keep you all informed. As of this moment, forty-five structures in Deadwood have burned and firefighters are battling several more. The fire is still out of control and more recruits are arriving as I speak."

~ ~ ~ ~ ~

As soon as a new song starts playing on the radio, Mom and Aunt Dolly turn to the television for the

10:00 news.

Glenda Watkins is reporting on the fire in Deadwood, "Governor Ralph Herseth has ordered seven National Guard units from around the Black Hills into action. He also contacted Governors Hickey of Wyoming and Davis of North Dakota for assurance of national help if needed. The American Red Cross is providing food and a make-shift resting place for weary firefighters at the courthouse.[15]

"Men are blackened with the soot and ash from burning timber. Firefighters work desperately to douse the houses on fire, in Deadwood and along the highways that are engulfed in flames. Volunteers use their own tools. They share shovels, axes, and hoses to work the fire.

"Soon, there will be almost four thousand fire fighters working side-by-side to put out this terrible blaze. The fire has surrounded Deadwood on THREE SIDES! And has lit up the night like a candelabra! Soot and cinders have ruined clothes and ignited hundreds of smaller fires, which home owners and townspeople have valiantly put out," she continues in a scared, excited voice. Glenda gasps or coughs occasionally, but does not stop in her dramatic rush of words. "Many houses in Deadwood have burned to the ground! Patients from Deadwood have been moved to the Homestake Hospital in Lead.[16] Here's hoping they won't have to be moved again." Her hair is disheveled. Her cheeks and eyes are bright red which makes her look a little drunk.

The other newscaster at the station breaks in and says, "Wow, Glenda. Are you alright? Is there a danger to your personal safety?"

"No, Richard. I'm fine here at fire control central in the Franklin Hotel, downtown Deadwood." She makes a show of coughing. "But, let me tell you that the air is so dense here that walking down the streets in this downtown area is truly dangerous. My eyes have been irritated since I got here. But, for those fighting the fire, it is even worse!" She catches her breath and finishes, "This is Glenda Watkins, reporting from downtown Deadwood, where a wild fire rages out of control through the Black Hills of South Dakota. Signing off for KRSD Channel 7, in Deadwood, South Dakota."

11

Asthma Morning

I cannot remember going to bed, but it is morning and I get up because I hear the sounds of Mom having an asthma attack. She wheezes in and out, to her own very unsteady rhythm. When I get to the kitchen, she is sitting at the table with a coffee cup in front of her, gasping as her chest heaves. The morning news reports the fire is seventy-five percent contained and is going north, so Lead will probably be saved.

Aunt Dolly says, "Hey! I heard the fire is almost under control, and we probably won't have to evacuate." She puts her hand on my shoulder and seems glad to be able to share some good news.

Mom struggles to say, "I just . . . cannot (wheeze) do it today . . . You (gasp) kids will have . . . to help . . . get (wheeze) stuff done. Annette, . . . can you (gasp) bring me . . . my cigarettes?" She points to where her pack of Pall Malls and lighter are on the counter.

I mutely grab the cigarettes and lighter, plus an ashtray from the side table, then bring them to Mom.

Why does she want a cigarette now? I just can't

stand this. I can't understand why she wants to smoke when she can't even breathe . . . I hate listening to her wheezing and gasping.

"Betty, . . . make (wheeze) the kids . . . some . . . breakfast . . . (gasp) will you?" Mom says, breathlessly.

"Oh, Anne, I'll make the breakfast," Aunt Dolly breaks in. She has been holding baby Mark on her lap, but she gets up and places him in his highchair.

Stop talking. Stop talking! I can't take that sound of struggling air. I need to get away!

I slip into the bathroom for a moment of escape, closing the door firmly behind me, as I hear Betty say what I cannot.

"Yes, Mum. You can save your breath for breathing. I know precisely what to do," Betty says as gently as possible. When Mom is like this, Betty's voice gets softer and very formal. She begins to use full sentences and talk like she is British. It's because she hates to hear Mom try to talk during an asthma attack.

As I return to the kitchen, Mom looks at us with an intense look of accusation, as if we are the reason for her lack of air. We are terrified of Mom—and for Mom—when she has asthma attacks. There is nothing we can do for her. And yet she asks us to be strong, to be available, to do the work, and hardest of all to be witness to her labored struggle.

I bet Dad feels like this today too, with all the smoke he is breathing in, fighting the fire. What if he begins having asthma attacks too. Oh! I will not be able to live with them both gasping. Good grief!

Actually, we are all breathing heavy, coughing and gasping, so Mom's *asthma music* is amplified by many of us kids' coughs and wheezes. It's scary to have that "I can't breathe!" feeling, even a little bit. We can all relate to Mom's suffering today in this new way. It adds to our scared feeling.

"Will we havta' go to school today?" Lenny asks, rubbing his eyes as he comes in. His hair is still disheveled from sleep. He has heard what Aunt Dolly said and is wondering the obvious. Lenny, like everyone else, sounds hoarse.

"No. No school today. You will all get a holiday and return to school tomorrow, I suppose," Aunt Dolly answers.

"Yeah! No school!" Ronny cheers as he comes into the kitchen, then stops abruptly as he looks at Mom intently. He strolls to the toaster and quietly puts a slice of bread into it, then stands as if at attention.

Aunt Dolly gets the big stock pot from the cupboard and Betty hands her the box of oatmeal. Dolly starts pouring water into the pan and the two of them get the breakfast made, almost silently communicating what each one needs to get oatmeal and toast for the rest of us.

Mom, in her halting manner and labored breathing, asks David to turn the television on even though she has been listening to the radio. We kids skulk around the room, eat breakfast, and listen for any news about the fire. I pray that Mom will stop gasping and breathe normally soon.

Please God, let us all start breathing normally—soon!

~ ~ ~ ~ ~

"The fire is furious and relentless. Up one mountainside and down the other, it rides the hills like a roller coaster. It seemed to burn faster as the sun went down last night and the efforts to subdue it seemed impossibly feeble," Glenda Watkins is back on the air.

She's in a new outfit, but her hair looks like it's been singed. She has dark circles under her red eyes. "The men and women of Deadwood, Center City, and Pluma are determined to save their homes! They fight the good fight of people armed with a love for the land and their families. The fire department has been hosing down houses along the north and east sides of Deadwood, but it has been a losing battle. They are worn, weary, and exhausted! The Lead, Sturgis, and Custer fire departments are working as well. We all hope they will get the building fires under control."

"Boy, I sure hope my brother Roger's home is not one of those burning," Aunt Dolly says softly.

Cousin Doreen pats her mom's arm and goes over to stand by her. "It'll be okay, Mom," she says.

"The fire is like a stubborn stallion that will not be put in its stall. It bucks and yawns at the firefighters' attempts to extinguish it. It rears back and rages in one place, then another. Once it is out, a spark ignites the fire again and more water or dirt is needed," Glenda continues in a very animated way, like she must have seen it with her own eyes. She is inside this morning and the other announcer casts scared looks her way. They are showing still photos of the forest on fire and men fighting the flames.

"Boy, she sure is energetic this morning," Lenny observes.

"Yeah. She's flamboyant," Ronny says with a smile. "Get it? Flame-boy-ant!"

"Flame-boy-ant!" Richie repeats.

"Ha ha. She's flamin' all right," Doreen says. "It looks like she got too close to the fire last night. Her hair is sure frizzy."

"Yeah. Someone should hose her down. I bet she's had about a thousand cups of coffee since last night," Aunt Dolly replies. "She looks like she could be wired for sound."

"Is it the sound of fire?" Lenny wants to know, but his joke is only funny to him.

"She's burning with the desire to broadcast," says Ronny. Then he and Lenny punch each other in the upper arm and laugh.

"A hunka-hunka-burnin' love," David says and swivels his knees in an Elvis impersonation. Richie repeats David's "Hunka-hunka-burnin' love!" and they both start swiveling their knees and getting into a short knee and hip swiveling contest.

"Ha!" Mom barks, then wheezes as she tries to suck in more air. The boys all go mute. We all look around at each other, still smiling because the boys WERE pretty funny, but with Mom breathing like that, we also get the seriousness of the moment. We go back to eating breakfast.

"But, when does Dad come?" Valerie wants to know. "I miss him." That sentiment sinks in quickly with the whole gang and we all think of Dad and what he might be doing.

"We all miss him, sweetie," Aunt Dolly says. "Do we know anything more about Uncle Roger? How is he?" Betty asks out loud.

"I just don't know. I don't think there's been any update on the news either," Aunt Dolly replies. She shakes her head a little and brushes a tear from her eye.

The phone rings. Aunt Dolly hurries to answer it. It's her husband, Uncle Ralph calling to see how we are doing. He is in Omaha taking care of his own mother who was hospitalized from a stroke. Aunt Dolly hears the progress from him, tells him to stay put with his mom and that the family is okay, for now. There is nothing he can do to help our situation and he is one less person for her to worry about. I can see her face scrunch up to cry, then straighten out again after a deep breath. She looks like it takes effort to keep the tremble out of her voice. Silent tears fall down her cheeks the whole time she is on the phone. When she is done, she quickly goes into the bathroom to compose herself. When she comes out, she brushes her hair back with her hand and smooths her apron.

Later, while Betty and I are doing the breakfast dishes, I say quietly, so no one else will hear, "I just hope Dad is alright. And Mom. I hate it when she gets this way. It's so scary. What if Dad gets asthma too? What if both Mom and Dad die? What would we do, then?"

Betty suggests we pray the 23rd Psalm together. We quietly recite the Psalm, then continue in whispers discussing the "yea, though I walk through the valley of death" part saying, "Dad is probably fighting the fire in the valley of death." And we say an extra prayer for him.

~ ~ ~ ~ ~

At KDSJ, Harry has stayed on the air all night long relaying evacuation instructions and updating listeners with the latest news.

"Lead will most likely not have to evacuate. The fire is eighty percent contained,"[17] he says, as he surveys the blackened forest around the station through his picture window. The smoke has cleared somewhat from the station during the night and the temperature has dropped to a still uncomfortable ninety-six, yet it feels like a balmy evening compared to what he has been experiencing. The haze continues to burn his eyes, but he has water and he's sure he'll have enough to make it to the next day. He has eaten the sandwich he brought for yesterday's lunch—the only food available to him, and is listening to the growl of his stomach along with the music and commercials. Mom and Dolly hang on Harry's every word and sigh at each break for songs that they would normally enjoy hearing and singing along to.

"I'll keep updating you all as I get more information, but for now, let's take a trip down memory lane with this golden oldie, 'Mona Lisa' by Nat King Cole. This is Harry Daniels in the smoke and the soot, past the blaze and in the haze, from the hottest spot in the Black Hills (He makes a hissing sound like hot steam coming off a teapot)—coming to you, LIVE, from KDSJ!"

We kids all smile. Aunt Dolly gives Mom a hug. Then Mom and Aunt Dolly listen, drink coffee, and smoke cigarettes.

"Do you think we should begin unpacking the car?" Aunt Dolly asks.

"Let's . . . wait . . . a little . . . while. (wheeze) Just in case," Mom gasps, and she sits at the table struggling to breathe. Even us big kids know there is the chance the "Don't Evacuate" order could be reversed. We won't be safe until the fire has been fully put out. Housework has stopped as Mom and Aunt Dolly cannot focus on anything but the immediate, which is us kids and preparing—or waiting to evacuate or not evacuate.

Panic keeps Mom's asthma attack going longer

than it might have. The heavier, smoky air, the anxiety about Dad, and the worry about evacuation have taken their toll. She is now battling the consequences of their combined assault with a full-blown asthma attack that has been going on since before we all got up.

"When will Dad come home?" Charlie asks.

"Yeah, Mom. When will Dad come?" Valerie echoes Charlie.

"I don't . . . know. (Wheeze) I . . . just . . . don't know," Mom answers. She takes a sip of coffee and clutches her inhaler.

~ ~ ~ ~ ~

Even though the fire has been contained and is eighty percent out, many men are still working very hard to finish the job. Dad is in a crew that has worked its way up a steep incline, felling trees and cutting brush, then shoveling dirt over that to dampen the burning. The fire is still very intense for them.

Suddenly they hear a roar, sounding like a locomotive, raging toward them. The air becomes heavy with the smell of burning wood and it becomes instantly harder to breathe. Dad pulls his bandana more snuggly over his nose and squints into the smoky forest. He gasps as he tries to take a deep breath and wipes his head with his handkerchief as he looks around for the next area to cover with soil. Finding what he's looking for, Dad begins again.

The breeze dies suddenly. The air is absolutely still. Dad looks up, holding his shovel full of dirt. His eyes open wide and he yells, "Firestorm's coming! RUN!" And he begins to race down the hillside. Those men around Dad all run down the hill toward a stream of water that seems too small to help at all. They dive into the water as the fire flashes over the hill they were just on seconds before. A couple men don't get completely under the water in time, and their clothing bursts into flames.

12

Being in Charge

It is early afternoon, just after lunch. The three youngest kids have just been put to bed for naps. We older kids are playing a lackluster kickball game outside and trying to stay quiet about it. Since there is no school today because of the fire, we welcome the chance to get out of the house and away from Mom's wheezing even though it is hot and very smoky outside. The air is dense and thick with flakes. It could be snowing, but the stuff falling is not white. Despite that, we are trying to play kickball.

"Okay, your turn, Betty. Git us a homer," Lenny says.

"Yeah! Git a homer," repeats Richie.

Doreen tosses the ball toward home plate. She is tall for her age and as capable as any nine-year-old boy. Her dark hair is cut short and matches her dark eyes. Everyone calls her a "tomboy" and she is proud of it. Her athletic build helps her run as fast, climb as high, and send baseballs over the fence as good as most boys—better than a lot of them. Today, like most days,

Doreen is the pitcher.

Betty kicks at the ball, hits it, but hits a rock too. "Oh, ow! Ouch! OW!" she screams. "That really hurts! Now you broke my toe!" and she hops around on her other foot in tears. Doreen and I grab her on either side and help her hop into the house. The game is stopped as the other kids try to figure out what just happened. There is a fairly large rock sticking up from the ground. Like an iceberg, most of it is under the surface, but enough of it is up so that if you kicked it, you would hurt yourself.

The ball had miraculously rolled right over the rock at the same instant Betty kicked; and her toe had not only hit the rock, but damaged the ball so that now there is a two-inch tear in it. The ball rapidly deflates, and the kickball game is kaput.

"What did she kick?" Richie asks.

"The ball had something in it," David says.

"That can't even be true. It's inflated. The only thing in there is air," Lenny responds.

"No, she kicked a rock," Ronny says.

"I didn't throw a rock. I threw the ball," Doreen says, having come back out to get the ball and feeling like she needs to defend herself.

"The rock is that one that sticks up from the ground," Ronny says. He walks over to it and gently kicks it with the toe of his shoe.

"How could the ball roll over a rock?" Stevie asks.

"I don't know. I threw the ball just like always," Doreen says, yelling a little.

"Well, that is a very peculiar thing," says Richie who has just learned the word peculiar and wants to use it all the time, now.

The other kids follow Doreen back into the house and watch Aunt Dolly look at Betty's toe. They are not silent, however, as everyone expresses his or her opinion about the kick, the ball, and the rock.

"Well, . . . what else . . . can . . . happen (wheeze)?" Mom gasps in exasperation. After a short discussion, Mom and Aunt Dolly decide Betty had better see a doctor and that if Mom goes along, they might help her too. Mom and Betty get into the car, with me helping Betty hop along toward the passenger side, and Aunt Dolly helping Mom get into the driver's side. Mom moves slowly, leaning heavily on Aunt Dolly and stops often to take breaths. We all watch and wait for her. She manages to get into the car, but cannot breathe enough to start the car's engine.

"Oh, for heaven's sake!" says Aunt Dolly. "You cannot drive in this condition. Just get over. I'll drive!"

"But who'll stay with us kids?" Doreen asks her mom, raising her voice in alarm. All of the rest of us stop in our tracks, our worry spreading as quickly as the forest fire. In an instant, we are all standing around Aunt Dolly, staring up at her in expectation.

"Well," Aunt Dolly stops for a second and looks around at us kids. "Annette, you are the oldest. I'm putting you in charge of the gang, here. Doreen, you're second in command. You other kids better listen to Annette. She's the boss now. Be good until we get back!"

"Annette, you are in charge, now," Aunt Dolly says to me as she puts an arm around my shoulders and gives me a you-can-do-it squeeze.

"Hey, I'm second in command. I have some 'in charge' too," says Doreen.

Aunt Dolly nods and says, "I expect you do and you will be, Doreen. And, I expect you all to cooperate with Annette," as she looks around, pointing her fingers at Ronny, Lenny, David, and Richie. Then she gets into the car with Mom and Betty and takes off to the hospital. We all stand stock still, in surprise as they drive out the long driveway and turn onto the street.

I think I'm gonna' pass right out! How could she leave us here all alone? What was she thinking putting me in charge of one, two, three, four, five, six, seven, eight, nine, ten, ELEVEN! Eleven? Eleven kids! Are you kidding me? I'm in charge?!

I look around at all the faces looking right back at me. Many of them have their mouths wide open. I snap mine shut quickly and gulp the lump in my throat back down.

Are you kidding me?

"Hey! They can't 'vacuate and leave us here!" yells Stevie, who has not followed the fast-moving events. Becky hears Stevie and begins to run after the retreating car, crying as she goes.

"Stevie, Mom is just taking Betty and your Mom to the hospital. They'll be back for us," says Doreen, holding him by the shoulders so he pays attention.

I run after Becky and stop her. Then I say, "They'll come right back, Becky. They are just going to the hospital to fix Betty's foot." We trudge back to the waiting group while I furiously think of how to be in charge.

"Okay, okay. Let's see. We can do this. Right? Huh? What do ya' think? We can stay together and be okay without them here. You guys will help me, right?" I look at Doreen and Lenny and Ronny. They nod their heads in unison.

"I can help ya with the little ones," Doreen says. "We are almost the same age, so I'll help."

"I'll help ya, sis," Lenny says.

"Yah. You got my vote," Ronny adds.

David and Richie nod in agreement, looking like a couple of bobble-heads.

"I want to help too!" chimes in Becky who has calmed down and now wants us to know she can help. She gets a hug from Doreen.

"Hey. I kin help," Valerie says coming over to the girl huddle.

"Yeah. We will all work together," I say as tears spring to my eyes and I try to hide them. I feel a tiny bit less panicked and take a deep breath and blow it out, to keep my tears inside. I fix a smile on my face. I feel like Mom—what else can go wrong? Mom AND Aunt

Dolly have just left with our only way out of this town. I hope the TV or radio announcers don't reverse their good news and declare an evacuation before Mom and Aunt Dolly come back from the doctor's office. Being the boss feels lonely and scary, even with Doreen as second in command and all the offers of help from the other kids.

"How about if each of us older kids takes a younger one to be in charge of? Do you guys think you could do that?" I ask as long as everyone is still standing around looking at me like a bunch of lost puppies.

"Okay, yeah," says Lenny and the other kids nod their heads.

"Okay, I say," warming up to my plan. "Lenny, you take Charlie. Ronny, you take Ralphie. David and Richie, can you play with Stevie? Doreen, can you watch Becky and Valerie? They always play together anyway. I'll take baby Mark, 'cause he'll need his diaper changed. Unless anyone objects to that." I wait for them to think about my plan. Then, I realize I have to give them something to do as well.

Boy! Some folks sure need direction.

"Let's figure out what you can do to pass the time. I'll think about what to make for supper too," I continue.

"Oh! What happens if the little kids fight with us?" David wants to know.

"Aw, Dave, you can handle Stevie. Just put him in a headlock!" Lenny laughs.

"No. No headlocks and no fighting!" I say, raising my voice a little. "Mom will kill us if we were fighting while she was at the hospital. Let's all just get along."

I suggest to Doreen that she and the two younger girls go inside and read while they wait for Mom and Aunt Dolly to come home. None of us knows what will happen next and that part is the scariest of all.

The boys decide to trade the kickball game for trucks and look for the broom we use to sweep roads into the dirt. David goes to get the trucks, as Stevie yells, "I call the Tonka!" It looks like they are off to a pretty good start.

The smoke seems like a heavy curtain. The acrid smell and the bits of debris makes my eyes sting and burn, makes my throat raw and scratchy, and keeps the urgency to flee front and center. All of us kids have begun to really gag and cough this second day of breathing the smoke-laden air, and our eyes are rimmed with red. I think I'd better have them all go inside pretty soon.

Let's go. Let's just go. Until the fire is over, let's just get out of this smoke.

I walk down the long driveway to the street and back again to try to settle down. My siblings one by one, at different times, have done the same. We each feel the need to flee—to get away from the ever-worsening air, the smell, and the smoke, even if the fire is being contained. The cars passing down the street are fully loaded, and I feel more scared and lonely than ever.

After some time outside, breathing is truly hazardous. I ask the boys who have lingered in the yard to join the girls inside the house. I get baby Mark out of bed, change him and give him graham crackers for a snack.

Doreen is playing school with the two little girls who are arguing over the crayons. Lenny, Ronny, Ralphie, and Charlie are playing cards, but the little boys can't figure out the rules and Ronny is yelling at them.

"Okay, okay, you guys. What's the deal here?" I ask trying to sound casual. "Ronny, you know these two aren't old enough to understand the rules, much less play by them. Let's cut 'em some slack, okay?"

"Yeah. Yeah. Yeah!" Ronny sounds angry. He wipes his hands down his pants and takes a deep breath.

"Hey!" Lenny says. "Let's build houses with cards. Here. I'll show you guys how to stack one on top of two." Lenny starts stacking cards.

"Thanks, Lenny," I say softly in his ear, and I move to Stevie, David, and Richie wrestling on the living room couch and floor.

I send them into the cupboard under the stairs to change their game. It is a triangle space with one wall angled from the underside of the stairwell. The other two walls are straight, so if you sit next to the west wall, you can sit up all the way. We always let the biggest kid, whoever it may be, sit against the tall wall. The cupboard houses a variety of toys. If you push the scattered toys to the edges, there is room for several of us to sit inside. A dim bulb lights the area and, when the door is closed, there is a certain amount of quiet and privacy. For a while they play with puzzles. Then the boys get antsy and begin to wrestle again.

"Now, David and Richie, I'm gonna need you to help me here. How can you three play without being so rowdy? What can ya' do?" I stand with my hands on my hips, giving them my most mom-like stare and wait them out.

Finally, David says, "Okay. How 'bout we build with blocks. Can we go under the kitchen table and build a fort?" We have an odd assortment of wooden blocks that are kept in the basement in an old laundry basket. Every time Dad makes something using a two by four, he cuts one or two more blocks for us. It's our job to sand the edges down, which could be an activity in itself, except no one wants to work that hard. So, the blocks are a bit rough around the edges, but they work pretty well for play.

"Yep. That could be a good idea. Let's see if it is." I smile at him and give them the thumb's up sign. He and Richie run to the basement to get the basket while Stevie heads under the kitchen table.

After the boys leave, the three girls retreat to the space under the stairs and gather dolls to play "evacuation." They gather and fold all the clothing, wrapping everything up in a cloth napkin. There is one doll bottle and they take turns feeding dolls from the "magic" bottle, which empties as it is tipped up and refills when it is put down again. I help baby Mark gather up his trucks and push them back and forth to him.

It is surprising to me that we have passed the last bit of afternoon in quiet play. It is a long time waiting, being kind, being patient, solving problems, and worrying about Dad and Uncle Roger, Mom and Betty. Not knowing where they are or when they will be home is the hardest. I'm tired of being in charge. The weight of responsibility lies on my shoulders like a sodden, woolen blanket. I am tired of watching my siblings and cousins, of thinking up things to keep them entertained, playing their baby games, and problem solving when they squabble. I am tired of worrying. I just want to lie down and cry. But I push through it to carry on. I go to the refrigerator to see what food is there, then to the cupboard. I remember Mom had us make all those peanut butter sandwiches and put into the car. I head outside to retrieve them and remember Aunt Dolly drove the car to the hospital. I stop and stand still, stumped.

Sheesh! Now what? Okay. What do I know how to make? Let's see. Grilled cheese? No bread. Scrambled eggs and toast? No bread. Soup? Probably not. I can make pancakes! I know how to do that.

I spring into action once I get back into the kitchen. First, I look into the refrigerator. There are eggs and milk, so that's good. I go to the cupboard and find the box of pancake mix. Great! We are in business. I get out the large cast iron frying pan, a bowl, and big spoon and I begin to mix up pancakes. Then I remember Mom always gives us fruit or something with the pancakes. I look in the fridge for oranges or apples, but the fruit is gone. It's all in the car.

Wait! Chokecherries!

"Hey, Lenny, Ronny. Can you guys come over here a minute?" I ask in a quiet voice, so the other kids don't notice. "I was wondering if you guys could pick a bowl of chokecherries really quick so we could have them for supper? I'm pretty sure Mom either froze the ones you picked last night or they're in the cooler in the car."

They both grin and say, "sure 'nuf!" They take the bowls I hand them and slide out the door, along with their two tag-a-longs. Pretty quick all four are back inside coughing and smiling with bowls full of cherries, which I rinse and set on the table.

"Thanks! You're my heroes," I say with a smile. "Now, get a big glass of water to wash the smoke from your throats," which is a repeat of what Aunt Dolly has been saying for the last 24 hours. After I start the heat under the frying pan, I pull plates down from the cupboard and set a dozen plates around the table. I put forks out and glasses. When the frying pan is hot, I start making the pancakes. As soon as the other kids smell me cooking, they come into the kitchen looking pretty hungry.

"Oh boy! Pancakes!" Richie says.

"Yeah. I love pancakes," says Stevie.

"Well, you'll just have to wait while I cook them," I say, "Hey, David, could you get the syrup from the fridge, please?"

David looks in the refrigerator, but he cannot find anything. I go to the fridge and look as well. No syrup. I see a jar of jelly and take that out.

"Okay. I'll make some syrup, too. But we do have jelly and honey," I say, then I flip the pancake like Mom showed me how to do. I go to the cupboard and get a small saucepan, put in the butter and brown sugar with some maple flavoring. I begin to heat it up over a low flame. Doreen helps the younger girls get washed and up to the table without asking me. The bigger boys help the younger ones wash and everyone starts eating or waiting for pancakes. I'm thankful they are patient and that they even eat the pancakes that get cooked a bit too much.

Pretty soon, all the kids have mouths full of pancakes. Some kids use jelly or honey instead of homemade syrup. I am proud that I cooked and no one was grumpy about it.

They eat quickly and escape back to playing. Lenny and Ronny wash the other boys up after they eat and take them into the living room to watch television. Doreen takes the girls.

I look at the table, which is a war zone of spilled

sweets, tipped cups, and dirty plates. But I smile and start clearing the dishes into the sink.

Baby Mark gurgles in his highchair. I wash his face and hands and give him a toy to play with while I move around the kitchen. He is so sweet that he will sit there playing, babbling, and smiling while I talk to him and get the dishes done. I suppose I could ask the others to help, but they are watching each other and this feels more peaceful. So, I just get the kitchen cleaned up and coo at baby Mark.

And that's when the lights go out. "Oh. Good grief!" I say, and go to the light switch, flipping it a couple times to confirm. The kids all race in.

"NO LIGHTS!" Lenny shouts, and Richie echoes with "NO LIGHTS!"

"The TV's died. It's a gonner!" says Ronny. "No 'lectricity!"

"Well, I know," I say in exasperation. "We'll be okay. I'll find a couple candles and we can read to the little kids by candle light. It'll be like we are pioneers."

"OH, and we can tell ghost stories," Doreen adds. I'm not so sure about that, but I say nothing.

There isn't much time for me to feel scared, because I know I must go right now to the basement for the flashlight, the emergency candles, and box of farmer matches. Yet, fear snuggles up and down my spine, cuddling me like a new bathrobe. I cannot share that fear with the other kids. Sweat breaks out on my neck and arms. I brace myself while slowly moving down the hallway. I silently pray as the evening light narrows. Gingerly, I step into the basement murkiness. I reach for the light cord, but of course there is no light. The darkness is a physical thing, pressing itself against me, hugging me until I can hardly breathe.

Muffled sounds become acute. I feel the breeze from the far door which is closed, but drafts easily. The dank, mildew smell of the cellar sneaks up and grabs me. I swoon, then reach my hand out and grab the side of the shelving unit. I hang on until my vision clears. Yes. I am afraid. I wear a salt-laced fear of the dark like a second skin.

I will myself to take measured, steady breaths as my eyes slowly adjust to the limited light. Finally, I locate the flashlight, grab it, and turn it on. I quickly find the candles and match box, then exit the basement exhaling the breath I didn't realize I'd been holding. I almost cry with relief as I hurry away from that most dreaded space.

The house falls silent as darkness descends, much like the fine, heavy ash from the fire. It feels like we are under a blanket. As I strike the match, we all hold our breath. I light one, two, three candles and line them up in the center of the table. I hear several others exhale as one. The smaller children's eyes light up as they gaze at the three flickering flames. Here we are waiting to evacuate the forest fire, yet creating our own small fire right inside the house.

The candles create a blurred edge to everything around the room, casting shadows and sculpting ridges and planes not seen before. Small sounds, like a dripping water faucet, seem louder. Even small movements echo absurdly.

It is not yet full-on dark, but the lack of electricity and the dimming sunlight, which has already been reduced by the smoke and ash, make the early evening seem much later. My ears stretch in the darkness. I listen—really listen, to the dimming light. It seems my siblings and cousins are doing the same. They were all silent as I returned from the basement. The light from the candles makes the darkness creep nearer to us and, for a moment, we begin to huddle into the circle the candle flames have created.

Now, it's like we all slowly wake up and begin to murmur. Lenny and Ronny pick a book from the pile they have brought to the table. They sit, shoulders touching as near to the candle as possible while they take turns reading. Pretty soon, several voices can be heard softly reading and all eyes are on one book or another. The little girls have the deck of cards and are building card houses.

I look around and see that peace has come to our band of abandoned children. We can be busy and mostly content while the fire rages around us.

Well, like Tiny Tim in Christmas Carol, 'God bless us, everyone.'

13

Tea Time

It is after 6 p.m. I have finally just finished putting the dishes away when Aunt Dolly brings in Mom and Betty, whose foot is wrapped. Now, everyone crowds around them.

"Oh! Wow! What did the doctor say? Is it broken? Is it your toe or your foot? Wow, what a big bandage! Are the crutches yours? How long will you need to use them? Can I try out the crutches? Did you cry? Are you in pain?" the kids ask a hundred questions as Betty comes in on crutches and sits carefully down at the table.

Mom has gotten a shot or some kind of medicine and is no longer wheezing. But, at first, we don't notice Mom because all eyes are on Betty. The crutches are fascinating and several of the boys try them out.

"My big toe is broken. What did you put in that kickball?" Betty complains.

"You didn't hit anything in the ball, Betty. You kicked the rock in the yard!" Doreen says.

"Yeah! It was a big rock. The ball rolled right

over it!" Richie yells because he is excited.

"Yeah. And the ball! The ball is ripped apart!" Stevie yells, too, and Aunt Dolly tells us kids to all settle down and use our inside voices, for heaven's sake.

"No. You guys put something in that ball," Betty responds, not willing to give up her idea yet.

"Honestly, I rolled the ball the way I always do. You kicked the rock, too," Doreen says once again.

"How come you kids are sitting here in the candle light?" Mom asks.

"Well, the electricity went out. I thought we should get some light before dark, and we decided to sit around the table so we could all see to read." I felt a little defensive, having to explain.

Aunt Dolly pats my shoulder and gives me a smile. Then, Mom says to me, "Go to the basement and get Dad's transistor radio so we can at least hear the news. And grab a couple more candles, as well."

I grab the flashlight and bring it, the candles, and the radio back almost immediately. Aunt Dolly lights a couple more candles and sets one by the stove and one by the sink. She gets the flashlight from me and hands it to Doreen. She tells Doreen to go get one of the loaves of bread and the package of cheese from the car.

Aunt Dolly spreads butter on the bread and makes three grilled cheese sandwiches. Pretty soon the boys, smelling that grilled cheese, want some too.

"I did just make pancakes for them, and they

ate a lot!" I tell Aunt Dolly and Mom.

"Yeah, and boys are always hungry," Aunt Dolly laughs. "Doreen, please run upstairs and see if we have any more cheese in the freezer. Bring that down, and I'll make a couple more sandwiches. You boys can split what I make."

The debate continues throughout the meal about whether someone put something into the ball, or if Betty really did kick the rock. There is no real conclusion and it is a moot point because, either way, her toe is really broken and the ball is still a dud.

Finally, we all settle back down. I'm grateful that Aunt Dolly, Betty, and Mom are back. Somehow, I feel almost whole again, and lighter, too.

After second supper, we are all pretty listless. We just lay around the living room. There is nothing to do. We do not want to read by candlelight anymore. We do not want to play cards or any of the few board games we have. Now that Mom and Aunt Dolly are back, even the younger kids are quarrelsome and bored. The waiting and wondering is taxing everyone. Our eyes and throats are scratchy. The air feels heavy and full of things—which it is. It is full of forest particles so small you cannot see them and bigger ones the size of snowflakes. The smell of smoke is ever present and our panic, collectively and individually, escalates in the night air.

First one, then another of us asks, "When are we going to see Dad?" Staying feels like imprisonment as the air seems to get worse and the smell stronger. Our natural "flight or fight" response is near the surface for practically all of us kids, and Mom and Aunt Dolly, as well. The urge to flee has not left us, just because the fire marshal says we are no longer in danger. Even if Mom would pile us all into the car and drive us around town, it would help solve some of our angst.

Aunt Dolly forces herself to sit down so she will stop pacing. Mom listens intently to the radio. She knows full well that the announcement not to evacuate has been on several times and that the fire is almost under control. Since we have not heard from or seen Dad, Mom still feels she needs information. Now, because the electricity is off, it feels like we don't know enough, even though the transiter radio is providing up-to-the-minute information.

Because of the continued smoke and haze and the very real danger of another asthma attack, Mom is on edge. She clutches her inhaler in her hand. I see her think about, then decide not to use it. She puts it in her apron pocket, then takes it out again.

"If you kids don't quit moping around and find something to do, I will put you to work. There are mopboards to scrub in every room of this house," Mom announces to everyone, but no one in particular. She gets up grabs a rag and begins to scrub the kitchen sink.

"Mom, my froat hurts," Valerie says and stands at Mom's knee.

"It might be time for you all to just take a bath

and go to bed," Mom replies.

"Doreen and Annette, can you two please run the bath water and get the two little boys in the tub?"

"Can we take two candles with us?" asks Doreen. Aunt Dolly hands the big candle that sits on a catch plate to Doreen and I pick up the other big candle.

I trudge into the bathroom and begin running water.

Okay. Okay, now we'll spend an hour giving everyone a bath. Sheesh.

Still, doing something eases the tension of wanting to run away. Pretty soon I settle into the washing of two little brothers, Ralphie, and then my little sister.

Aunt Dolly sends the bigger boys upstairs to start taking showers. She has the shower upstairs and we have the tub downstairs, so the big boys take a shower by themselves, while we girls have to help the little ones.

"Aunt Dolly, we are going into your 'inner sanctum'," Lenny says with a grin.

"Well, just be sure you leave my 'inner sanctum' as clean as when you went in there. I will want to take a shower, too. And be careful with that flashlight!" she says, pointing her finger at him and giving Ronny her stern look.

"Okay, Mom," Ronny says. "Who's going first?"

"Me! I'm gonna do it. I'm heading into the IN-

NER SANCTUM!" Lenny says with a scary voice and both he and Ronny laugh a demented laugh.

"Just get a move on and don't use up all the hot water," Aunt Dolly says, more firmly.

Doreen and I bathe and towel dry the little boys, then send them to Mom and Aunt Dolly for pajamas.

"I want to take a bath all by myself," Valerie exclaims in her most haughty voice. Doreen and I are happy to have one less thing to do, so we sit on the bathroom floor and wait for her to take her own bath.

Becky wants to take a shower but her mom says no, she's still bath-taking age. She huffs around the kitchen a while and goes into the bathroom when Valerie comes out. After Becky is done, Stevie has to go in and he wants to take his own bath, too.

Boy, we've spent a lot of time on this bathroom floor, tonight!

Betty gets to comb hair, since she has to sit with her casted foot up. She combs Valerie's hair into curling pigtails and puts different colored ribbons on each. Then she combs Becky's strawberry blonde hair into a high, top knot and puts a ribbon in it. Becky sits up straight with a smile on her face.

Pretty soon we are all sitting on the couch with freshly combed hair and clean pajamas on, looking pretty damp, but clean.

"Mom, my froat is still scratchy," Valerie says to Mom, who looks a bit worried, and I realize we could all be headed for a few not-sick, but not-well days with all the smoke and soot in the air. I wonder if Mom will have another asthma attack or if we will all get asthma with the air so bad.

"Well. Hmm? It might be time for tea," Mom says. She looks around at all of us. "Now that you are all washed and clean, you kids look pretty spiffy. What say you find a hat and dress for tea? I'll put the kettle on!"

"Polly put the kettle on, we'll all have tea!" Aunt Dolly sings.

Us kids all smile and then scatter to find a hat or shawl or gloves. I find Mom's garden hat and feel like that is enough for me.

It seems quite romantic and cozy in the candle-light as we sit around the kitchen table. Mom places a cup and saucer in front of each of us. Doreen, Betty, and I each get one of Grandma's fancy teacups and saucers because we are old enough to not break them. At least, I hope I don't break it.

"I am Mrs. McGillycuddy," says Aunt Dolly in a falsetto voice. "Now, let's see who we have at tea today." She looks around the table at us expectantly. "Oh, I see we have Junior Anklebiter with us today," she says smiling and pointing to baby Mark.

"Tell me. Tell me!" says Ralphie.

"Oh. You are Mr. Kneeknocker. And there beside you is Mr. Ragamuffin." She smiles at Charlie. She goes around the table naming each of us with silly names.

David and Richie are the Looseknot twins. "David, you are Mr. Renegade Bandit Looseknot, and Richie is Cowpoke Horsewhip Looseknot." They grin and give each other a thumb's up sign.

"Valerie, you are Miss Rosie Lilacperiwinkle. And Becky is Miss Petunia Orangeblossom." Both girls smile and pretend to sip tea from their empty cups.

"Lenny, you are Mr. Blarney Stone Burpmagnet and Ronny, you are Mr. Aloysius Buttblower." She turns her smile to him, rubbing her hand over his hair.

Lenny lets out a loud fake burp and Ronny lifts his butt cheek and farts. Then we all say, "Peee-ewww!" and "Oh! geeze!" And they both laugh and then we all laugh.

Aunt Dolly says, "Oh, for heaven's sake!"

Mom comes around with the teapot. She has one towel over her forearm of the hand that holds the teapot handle. The other hand has a towel under the spout.

"Shall I pour?" she asks with a British accent, standing upright and proper.

"Yes! Pour me. Pour me," says Valerie. Since Mom is standing right next to her, she pours some in Valerie's cup and then into each of our cups around the table. We each get a graham cracker square. The squares have an indentation so you should be able to break them into two equal halves, but mine breaks into four small, ugly pieces and I leave it on my saucer. When baby Mark is done with his cracker, I feed him mine. I don't really like graham crackers anyway.

The tea is good. Mom made chamomile with a little lemon and honey. The sweetness soothes and the lemon seems to clear my nose.

We use phrases like, "Lovely tea!", "Thank you so very much!", "How are YOU today?", and "Very well, thank you." Aunt Dolly shows us how to lift the teacups with our pointer finger and thumb and keep our little finger in the air.

Richie slurps his tea. It's hot and he was blowing on it. But the slurp is loud and messy.

"Hey! You're not supposed to slurp tea," Becky says.

"Oh, on the contrary," Aunt Dolly replies with a smile. "Slurping is absolutely essential for tea! Here's how you do it." She blows across the top of her cup gently. Then ever so carefully, she touches her lips to the edge of the teacup and creates a loud slurp.

"Ahhhhh, simply splendid!" Aunt Dolly says.

The boys all start to laugh and shout. Then we all try slurping our tea and saying 'simply splendid!'

Mom and Aunt Dolly exchange looks and Aunt Dolly says to Mom, "We are gonna' have lots of kids wetting the bed tonight." Then, they both sigh.

After about half an hour, we are done with tea. The boys go back to the living room to sit and whisper ghost tales. Betty, Doreen, and I gather and wash up the cups and saucers.

"You kids should pick up a book and read by

candlelight. That's what our ancestors did," says Aunt Dolly, and moves to turn up the radio a bit. I think she is still wanting news and she would like us kids out of the way so she won't miss anything.

"Okay, let's play Slapjack with the little kids until bedtime," I say, and Doreen helps get our younger siblings to join in the game. Betty and the bigger boys sit around the table and attempt to stay focused on reading, often stopping to stare into space.

"Kids, it's bedtime. Give us a kiss and up you go," Mom says. She rises from her chair at the table and gets a bottle from the fridge for baby Mark. Then she picks him up and carries him into her bedroom to his crib.

Lenny lifts Charlie on his back. Ronny lifts Ralphie on his back and they go up the stairway.

"You kids all go to the bathroom good before getting into bed!" Aunt Dolly shouts up the stairs.

"Okay," Ronny shouts back down the stairs.

"Okay," Lenny echoes.

"I want a piggy-back, too," says Valerie.

"Well. You're too big for me to carry, Valerie. You'll have to just hold my hand," I say to her as we head to the bathroom, then go upstairs. Doreen has Becky right behind me.

"Annette, be careful with that candle," Aunt Dolly warns. The boys have the flashlight, so it's a candle for me and Doreen.

Becky and Doreen share the top bunk and Valerie and I share the bottom bunk of our shared bedroom. Betty gets the single by herself since she's the oldest, but pretty soon Baby Mark will join her. He's too little to pile in with the big boys just yet.

The boys have a similar arrangement with two sets of bunk beds in their room.

We older kids put our younger siblings to bed and say their prayers. But we want to stay up late again. The tea party has enlivened us and school has been suspended until after evacuation possibilities have passed, so Mom and Aunt Dolly reluctantly agree.

The news update on the radio has Glenda Watkins declaring her description of the fire. "Even though it is almost contained, the firefighters must continue to fight a blazing inferno! A later born wildfire burns as hot and intense as the original! The men are exhausted, yet courageous. Yes. These men who fight the wild fires have courage. It is not the courage of Superman, of Spiderman, or any Marvel comic book hero. Many men have been called from the Homestake Gold Mine to battle this blaze. These are the men who inhabit the mine's down under. They work in the belly of the earth and breathe the air beneath the surface. They labor willingly and steadfastly for their homes and their families. These are the men who live in Deadwood, Lead, Sturgis, Spearfish, Pluma, and Custer. They work day-in and day-out, every single day, every week, every month, for years to feed and clothe their families. They work to keep their homes safe and secure. They are the everyday heroes!"

She continues breathlessly, "They have the *'get-up-at-three-o'clock-in-the-morning, work-until-dusk'* kind of courage. They go to sleep only when the threat has passed. They work until the sinew of every muscle is depleted, past the breaking-point of exhaustion. It is the courage of men who have everything to lose if the fire wins this battle. They will not stop. They will not give in, nor give up, until every last timber is wetted and free from the threat of fire." She pauses for a brief moment and continues in her breathless, dramatic way.

We older kids, Betty, Lenny, Doreen, Ronny, and I have stopped what we were doing to hear Glenda as she recites her spirited report.

"She's really boring, Mom," Lenny says.

"No, she's not boring honey, she's theatrical," Mom explains.

"Yes. She's elaborating a bit too much," Betty adds.

"Yeah. And I'd say she's overacting by about a mile. But, she is eloquent in her description of our men folk," Aunt Dolly laughs.

They move on to a commercial and us kids lose interest. Still, I feel heavy. I cannot stop moving yet. I want to jump out of my skin. I cannot focus on anything. Even hearing Aunt Dolly say Glenda is theatrical, I cannot stop thinking she is right about our dads having courage. I want that kind of courage even if it is theatrical. Even a small amount of that kind of courage would feel alright in my book.

We kids sit around listlessly until we are told, one-by-one to go to bed. Finally, Mom, Aunt Dolly, and me are the only ones up. It is almost 11p.m. Mom and Aunt Dolly both talk about how worried they are for Dad and Uncle Roger. Mom has called the hospital to find out how he is but did not get anything more than, "stable."

"Dad is your brother, Aunt Dolly, but he's Mom's husband. Which is harder? To have your brother or your husband fighting the fire?" I ask, a little shyly, worried they will shush me.

"Oh, I don't know. I think it is about the same," Aunt Dolly says.

"I bet you are glad Uncle Ralph is in Omaha with his mom," I say.

"Yes. That thought has crossed my mind. Now, at least I don't have three men to worry about. Yet, I'm also concerned about my mother-in-law. She could easily have a second stroke. I sure hope she is on the mend, though," Aunt Dolly responds.

"Yes," Mom chimes in. "Uncle Roger is injured and we are worried about him. We also wonder how Aunt Jolene and the kids are doing, where they are, and if their house has burned down." She takes a puff of her inhaler. "And I wonder if Jolene even knows her husband is in the hospital."

"Well, I'm worried too. I was scared when you

couldn't breathe today. And, I was really scared when I was in charge," I say, in almost a whisper, tears welling up in my eyes.

"We just have to say a prayer and keep moving on. But you did a great job with the kids today. Thank you!" Mom says, putting her arm around my shoulder. "You're my big girl, aren't you?" I try not to let them, but tears begin to trickle down my cheeks and pretty soon I'm crying like a big baby. "We moms rely on our big kids, perhaps more than we should. Thank you for stepping up and managing," Mom says softly.

"Yes, Annette, you did a great job today taking over for us," Aunt Dolly says. Then she adds, "When I have a big job to do, when I'm worried, I say a prayer. Then, I think, 'What is the very worst thing that could happen?' and I figure out how I would go on, if it actually did happen. That way there is a plan—a thought, about how to continue."

"I try to keep busy doing things around the house. There is always something to do around here. But, it's still so hard to wait while not knowing about the people we love," Mom continues. She takes a drag from her cigarette and a sip of coffee. She pats my arm after setting her cup down again.

"Yeah," Aunt Dolly agrees, "it is definitely hard to stay here and wait. As John Milton said, 'They also serve who only sit and wait.'"[18] She recites the quote that is often said about and for the women who waited for their men to come home from war. I know it because she and Mom say it all the time to us, and we learned about it in school. But I am tired of waiting. I want to serve. I would rather be fighting the fire, or helping the injured, or doing something. Anything. I am just so tired of waiting.

They both gaze off into the distance like the other side of the room isn't something they see every day. I know that they are thinking about Dad and Uncle Roger and wondering as much as I am how they are doing. But both Mom and Aunt Dolly have ways to cope with their bad feelings, so I had better find some ways to cope, as well.

"You're tired, honey. It's been a long, long day. Why don't you go to bed?" Mom says. Finally, I get up, hug Mom and Aunt Dolly and slowly climb the stairs to bed.

14

Uncle Roger

"When will Dad come home? Will he come home this morning?" Lenny asks as soon as he gets up.

"I'm tired of waitin' for Dad. I want to see him," whines Valerie. She goes over and stands next to Mom, who gives her a little hug. Mom reminds us that Dad began work two days ago, worked all night, and worked all yesterday without much rest, if any. "He will be very tired and probably very dirty when he comes home," Mom says. She is looking pretty tired as well, and I see her put her inhaler to her mouth and suck in a big breath, hold it, and exhale slowly.

"Why isn't Dad home yet? The fire is over. He should come home now," David says, with a huff of impatience.

Then, Mom says, "I just don't know when Dad will come home. He may still be fighting the fire somewhere. Even though they told us we don't need to evacuate, the fire is still burning the forest, and perhaps parts of Deadwood. Or, he may be on his way home right now. Let's all try to be patient."

"Will we go back to school today?" Betty asks.

"I want to be home when Dad gets here," I say.

I can't even think about school right now. How can Betty be wanting to go to school? Sheesh.

"You can't be here to see Dad if you're in school," Lenny says.

"Can we stay home from school so we can see Dad?" David asks.

"We missed school yesterday. We should go today so we won't be so far behind," Betty says.

"Everyone else missed school, too. So how far behind will we be? We are all in the same boat," I retort.

"That's 'in the same forest fire'," Lenny says with a grin.

"The same forest fire," Richie echoes.

"There won't be school today. You will all go back tomorrow. They announced it at the top of the hour newscast. So, just relax, will ya," Aunt Dolly says, then fiddles with the antenna on the transistor.

The radio newscaster is talking about some men who have been injured by the fire. He calls on one of the men, whose name I don't catch.

"I was on a four-man crew working on a controlled burn at the edge of Highway 14. We were trying to burn off all the food for the fire by clearing trees. It's what's called 'firing out.' The natural boundary was the highway, but we knew that road was not gonna' be wide 'nuf to keep the fire from jumping across," a gravelly voice reports.

The radio announcer breaks in to tell us, "Fire-fighters look for a natural edge or boundary, such as a road, stream, or plain field, and they do a controlled burn between the barrier and the fire. This means that before the fire gets there, it would have already burned out."

"Yeah. Our natural edge was Highway 14. That was the plan, anyway. Bulldozers pushed down trees. Me and some other men used our saws to cut the branches off the trees. We were plannin' to light the trees on fire as soon as there was enough of a firebreak to keep the rest of the forest from catching fire, too," the man takes a shaky breath and coughs before he continues.

"I love the smell of the forest and I could clearly smell the pines and sumac trees in the area. I hate destroying the trees like that, but I know that it is a way to save the rest of the forest—and our homes! Suddenly, I heard a crashing sound and a tree was falling. My pant leg caught on a branch and I went down, then the tree fell on top of me," he finishes.

"You'd expect a person could get out of the way of a falling tree, but it's really harder than you think," the announcer says with a little chuckle. "And you were buried under the larger tree limbs, I understand. It took quite a bit to get you untangled from that tree! We're all glad you made it, Roger. Folks, that was Roger Stabnow, who is here in the Homestake Hospital surviving injuries from having a tree fall on him."

As he continues, the announcer says that the fire is ninety percent contained and shares the amount of forest that has burned: over four thousand acres. The radio goes to commercial break and the whole family, crowded around Dad's small radio, is left speechless.

"Did he say Roger Stabnow?" Aunt Dolly asks with eyes large. Her face has gone white. "Did he say it was Roger? I didn't recognize the voice at all. Do you think it WAS Roger?"

Mom hugs Aunt Dolly who is now, openly weeping. They discuss who will go to the hospital to see him, wondering if they can even get in. Should they call first?

What about Dad? Where is he? Is Dad one of the other injured men? That reporter didn't give us enough information!

Then Glenda Watkins is back to report. "The wind has died down, so less oxygen is being fed to the fire, and the burned trees and brush have been spent and used up so there is less fuel to burn.

"Most natural disasters, like this fire, will die of their own accord after a certain amount of time. But, leaving the fire to its own timeline means much more of the forest and many more homes would be burned. The heroic efforts of the many men who fought to diminish the amount of forest burned have helped reduce the time it takes before the fire is out and have certainly saved land, homes, and forest from the fire." Glenda Watkins is speaking in a dramatically solemn voice. She sucks in a deep breath and coughs some. She pauses to take a long drink of some beverage before she continues.

"By 9 a.m. some of the firefighters will be relieved, and a second battalion of volunteers will come in to renew the effort to finish dousing the remaining blaze. Containment has been sketchy all night. But as the winds die down and trenches hold, their efforts have become more successful." This she says in a more, cheery tone that sounds like there's a smile on her face.

"This is Glenda Watkins, signing off in Deadwood, South Dakota for KDSJ radio, where a raging forest fire has scorched over four thousand acres and destroyed sixty buildings, devastating this town!"

15

A Homecoming

Mom is making scrambled eggs at the stove. Her motions, even though she moves slowly, have a lightness in them that have not been there these past couple of days. I'm grateful that Mom is still well. It's hard to believe that it has only been two days since the forest fire began. It seems like years that we have been waiting and worrying, stuck in this smoky limbo-land. The air doesn't seem as thick today, but it still smells plenty smoky. We are all still coughing and blowing our noses constantly. Everyone is hoarse, but Mom more than the rest of us.

As the other children get up, they enter the kitchen and find a place to sit. Pretty soon the breakfast table is full of chattering, happy children with the prospect of a free day off of school.

After breakfast, dishes are done and the kitchen swept. Doreen, David, and I walk outside. The smoke on the northern horizon has widened considerably. As a matter of fact, it obliterates the northern and eastern horizon and, despite the already present smoke, additional haze oozes in our direction. Yet our immediate air seems clearer than it was yesterday. We hear and finally catch glimpses of airplanes flying around in the sky.

"I wonder where those helicopters are going?" David says as he follows the chopper with his eyes and pointed finger.

"Those aren't helicopters, they're air tankers," retorts Doreen. "And they're putting water on the fire.

"Nah. They're helicopters, and I knew about the water. I wonder which area they are goin' to. Will they be by Dad?" David says back at her.

"Well, they aren't putting water on the fire. They are putting slurry on it. I heard it on the radio," Lenny says, looking like a know-it-all. He and Ronny have joined us in the yard. Ronny nods his head in agreement with Lenny—two of one mind, as usual.

"Yep. Slurry," Ronny repeats.

"They are putting water on it too," Doreen retorts, and she and Ronny glare at each other, then they make room for Betty who has joined us, balancing on her crutches.

"I don't know what they are dropping, but I want a better look," I say and head for the pine tree. I'm feeling stronger somehow and more confident.

This time I'm gonna' climb as high as I can, to get a better look at that fire.

I begin the climb in the usual way by grasping the branch closest to the ground and hoisting myself up, using my feet on the trunk for balance. Once up on the first branch, it is very much like climbing a ladder, one branch at a time. As I climb, the smell of smoke intensifies blocking out the fresh pine scent I usually smell in the tree. My eyes, already scratchy, begin to tear up and I gag from the smoke that hangs in the tree. I can see the smoke as it hugs the ground, especially in the low-lying areas, but the view isn't much better than what I could see from the ground. The homes on the other side of the mountain that I could see last time I climbed the tree, are hidden by smoke today. I can only see Mae's home on the terrace below us, but nothing on Main Street.

I wonder what Dad can see as he fights this? How can mere mortal men overcome such a huge thing? Oh God, please keep Dad safe, and please help the men put out this fire!

I picture him and the other men, small and insignificant against the fire. The forest is so very big. But the fire has eaten up the forest, so it must be stronger. I have a new understanding of how really dangerous this forest fire is and I'm even more scared for Dad.

The breeze is more intense than the last time I was in the tree, but it is less gusty. The tree sways and I notice the narrowing width of the trunk. Even so, I easily manage to reach the tenth, eleventh, then twelfth branch. I see the air tanker dropping a dirty-looking something and another airplane that could be a helicopter circling in and out of the smoke, which swirls as it is affected by the 'copter. I look at the smoke on the horizon one last time before I begin to climb down.

Don't look down!

I focus my gaze at the tree trunk. But of course, I can't help but look down in order to begin my descent.

Suddenly, I hear the noise of a large truck in the street, its brakes squeal and gears shift. I look toward the street, trying to see it. Trees line the long driveway all the way to the street, but I am above them and can see part of the truck stopped in the street between the branches. All of a sudden, I see a grey-black figure getting out of the truck and beginning to walk down the driveway toward the house. He is almost unrecognizable. But I know the shape of him and the way he moves. I am certain it's Dad.

At first, looking down, I get the thrill of feeling scared and dizzy. My heart races and my breath catches in my throat. I have never been this high in the tree before. My head starts swirling and I catch my breath. But, knowing that Dad has been doing something very brave and knowing that he is home now, helps me to be brave, too. I descend the tree without thinking about it anymore. Even so, I breathe a sigh of relief when I touch the ground.

"Hey! You did it," Betty says quietly, and smiles at me, putting a hand on my shoulder when I get fully on the ground again.

"Yeah. I did it. It felt good, too," I say, then hurry toward the driveway. Betty follows me on her crutches, without knowing why I'm hurrying toward the street. I am the first to meet Dad halfway down the driveway. I fling myself at him and hug him with all my might. Dad is covered with soot and smoke. He smells burnt up.

"Hi!" Dad says, smiling a tired smile, and returns my hug.

Betty catches up and gives Dad a big hug, too. I grab Dad's lunch box and helmet and walk with him toward the house.

"What happened to you?" Dad asks Betty, seeing her crutches and bandaged foot.

"We had our own adventure, Dad. I broke my toe," she smiles at him. "I'll tell you about it later."

Dad is quickly greeted by shouting, laughing, smiling children. We are like a pack of puppies excited for supper—everyone talking at the same time. Dad looks so exhausted he can hardly walk, but the excitement of us kids invigorates him and provides the strength to keep walking, even though he has to be careful to not trip on anyone.

Dad walks in the house so surrounded by us kids that he has some difficulty getting through the door. He chuckles as he squeezes inside.

Mom sees us as we come in and she is at Dad's side in a blink. She kisses him, hugs him, and moves kids out of her way, so she can stand beside him.

Because us kids have all run to him, we are covered with soot and grime. His clothes are torn and singed. There are several burned spots and outright holes in his pants.

Wow, Dad looks terrible! He must be so tired. He looks burnt up—and thinner, somehow.

"Dad, you got dirt," Valerie exclaims.

"Soot! And dirt!" says Becky.

"Boy are you dirty!" Ronny exclaims.

"Boy are you dirty!" Richie echoes.

"Yeah, you're full of soot!" David says.

Stevie shouts, then jumps up and down with joy, shouting, "Dad's home! Dad's home!"

Valerie gives Dad's leg a hug and her blond hair turns immediately grey.

"Wow! Look at your helmet! It's melted," Ronny says.

"Wow! Your lunch box used to be tin. Now it's black!" yells Stevie.

"Your boots are black. Your clothes are black. You are all black!" says Richie in awe.

Mom says she will just throw his clothes away when he takes them off. And it looks like she'll have a lot of clothes to wash. We are all full of Dad's soot and grime.

"Dad, how was it? You look almost burnt up," Lenny asks in a quiet, concerned voice.

"Dad! Your eyebrows are gone!" Stevie says as he spies Dad's eyebrows. Normally, Dad has such bushy eyebrows that he can twist them into points. They look like devil horns when he does that. But, today, they are small, singed things, like short, shriveled up caterpillars.

"Wow!" say Lenny and Ronny. They are always up for adventure and are sure that Dad has some tales to tell. Everyone takes a turn to look at Dad's used-to-be-bushy, now-not-there, eyebrows. Then Aunt Dolly rushes in, takes Dad's face in her hands and kisses her big brother on each cheek. They hug, and suddenly it is a group hug. Now everyone carries some of Dad's soot on our clothing, face, and hands.

"Tell us about fightin' the fire, Dad," says Lenny.

We kids settle down to listen, feeling somehow comforted as we wear forest ash like badges from Dad. He tells us about fighting the fire and about taking breaks to eat and drink water. Then, looking at the boys, he talks about driving the bulldozer that listed sideways as he cleared the land for a firebreak.

"Yeah. My helmet and lunch box took a beating. I lost my thermos, though. Sorry, Babe," he looks over at Mom and she shrugs her shoulders.

"A small price to pay," she smiles back at him.

"I worked along-side other miners, digging a trench to create a break in the combustible forest material. The forest rangers had pulaskis, but we miners used the shovels and axes from working the mine. We were hoping to stop the fire from spreading further. The width of the roads did not stop the fire from jumping from one side to the other, so we were cutting a trench. We worked with other men to create a firebreak about one hundred twenty feet wide. The Ponderosa Pines are about eighty feet tall in that section of the forest, so the firebreak needed to be pretty wide," Dad said.

"What's a pul-ski?" Lenny asks.

"That's pulaski," says Dad. "It's like an ax with a double head, so you can dig and chop."

"We learned about the firebreak on the news this morning from Uncle Roger," David says and the other boys nod, knowingly.

"Wait. Roger was on TV?" Dad says and looks to his sister, Aunt Dolly.

"No. Well. He might have been. We think we heard him on your transistor radio," Aunt Dolly explained. "No electricity since last night."

Dad's story stops, while Mom and Aunt Dolly fill him in on Uncle Roger being injured, in the hospital, and being interviewed on the morning news. I am waiting, impatiently for them to get back to Dad's story.

I already know about Uncle Roger. What about Dad? What dangers did he survive? I want to hug him again, just because he is finally right here in front of us.

"Dad, will you get to stay home now that the fire is over?" asks Stevie.

"Oh no, son," says Dad, suddenly sober. "The fire isn't out yet. Not by a long shot. It'll probably take a couple more weeks for workers to get it all out and that's if we get some help from mother nature."[19]

"Well, who's fightin' the fire if you aren't doing it anymore?" Stevie says, and I bet he thinks Dad has single-handedly fought the fire.

"Oh, there are lots of forest rangers, National Guardsmen, regular firefighters, and there are still miners working on it. I expect there are lots of volunteers, too. I might be called to go back and fight it some more. I'll get a call to go to work or go fight the fire again," he reports.

"I hope they give you a chance to sleep a little," Mom says.

"Dad, are you gonna' finish telling us your story?" David asks, tugging his tattered pant leg.

"Yes. Tell about fightin' the fire," Richie says. Then he adds, "please," and looks up at Dad expectantly.

Dad rubs his hands over his face, smiles and takes a big bite of the scrambled eggs Mom has set in front of him. "Well, sure."

"This one time, a large flock of black birds rose up from the forest, spiraled, then raced past us men. A murder of crows. At least, I think that's what it's called. Good thing they were flying away, so they wouldn't be murdered, or burned up. The air was so hot it was like an oven!

"Other animals were running away from the fire, even as us men worked toward it. The darkened evening sky was lit up by the fire and I could see as well as if it was day. When the smoke was blowing at us, it covered and hid what we needed to see in order to stay ahead of the fire.

The deer and wolf race past on either side of Dad.

"Suddenly, a gust of wind blew smoke, debris, and heat toward us. We struggled to keep our balance on the uneven surface of the mountainside. The heat was like a hand pushing us back. Even though I was wearing my safety glasses, the smoke stung my eyes and small bits of burning embers made holes in all our clothes. The man next to me slapped at his beard, which flamed up and blackened. I joked and called him Blackbeard and he laughed back.

"Then there was a great crashing sound, and several animals ran out of the woods right at me. A ten-point buck jumped out from between two timbers directly in front of me. Right on its heels was the largest grey wolf I've ever seen! Both of them running blindly, fear shining in their eyes. They were so close I could see their *eyes*! And, I was so surprised that I could NOT move," Dad stopped and looked at us.

"Wow. That must have been so cool to see them so close like that!" Lenny said.

"Did you wish you had your shotgun, Uncle Bill?" Ronny asked.

"Weren't you scared?" asked Valerie in a whisper.

Dad looked at us kids, then kept going. "I just stared at those animals as they rushed at me. It happened so quickly I didn't have time to move. At the very last moment they parted and they ran past—on either side of me—creating a new wind as they went. They quickly disappeared. And you know what? I sat down on the ground. Hard."

Dad smiles and concludes, "I sat there for a couple minutes just in shock, I think."

"Tell us another, Dad!" said David.

"Yeah, tell us another," Richie repeated.

The boys all snuggle a little closer to Dad, as if that is even possible. Dad takes a bite of eggs and one bite of toast. Then he drinks some coffee.

He's stalling, thinking about what to say next. I bet some things are too scary to tell us. We probably should let him rest his voice a bit. Maybe he will want to talk more tomorrow. But, sitting with everyone, Dad so real and alive in front of us, just makes me want to stay here forever.

Dad begins another tale. His voice is almost as gravelly as Uncle Roger's. Mom comes over, puts her hand on his shoulder and bends down to rest her chin on Dad's head. When he begins again, she goes back to the sink, but turns around and looks at him while wiping the tears from her eyes.

"We saw several burned-up cars and a couple houses were blackened to sticks," Dad said. "The road was not wide enough to create a fire break so houses on either side were burned." Then he looked at our faces and stopped talking. He took another drink of coffee before he began again.

"This one time, me and my crew were on a steep hillside and I heard the roar of the approaching wildfire. The smell of burned timber was immediately stronger and the wind suddenly quit as if it was taking a breath. You know, the fire does that because the oxygen is so quickly used up. A thundering noise filled the air like a locomotive comin'. All the trees just burst into flames. We knew what was coming, but were helpless to stop it. I yelled at the others 'A firestorm is coming' and 'NOW!'" Dad stops and takes another drink of coffee.

"When I yelled to the others, I started runnin' downhill toward Little Strawberry Creek and dove into the water. I mean to say, we raced to that water! Then we all lay down in the creek and the fire blazed right over top of us with a whoosh. I kept my eyes wide-open. I still had on my safety glasses and they filled with water slow enough that I could see the fire rush over the water. I saw the firestorm dancing on the water and I held my breath for as long as I could, and then some!"[20]

"Dad, how did you stay under the water?" Lenny asks.

"Don't interrupt the story, Lenny," Betty says and she looks intently at Dad.

"Well, I just want to know in case I have to do that sometime," Lenny retorts.

"I grabbed a hold of the vegetation on the creek bottom so I would keep from breaking the surface of the water before the firestorm had passed," Dad explained. "That creek isn't that deep and we all had a time just staying under until the fire had passed."

Mom put her hands to her mouth and Aunt Dolly took in a breath we could all hear.

Dad and other firefighters racing to Strawberry Creek.

Ponderosa Pines: Days of the Deadwood Forest Fire

"Pretty soon we climbed out of the creek," he stops and looks around at us. "You know, a family of raccoons and several otters climbed out beside us and scurried away.

"'You okay?' I asked the man next to me, who nodded 'yes'. Then he asked me if I was okay. And we shook hands just grateful to be alive," Dad says. Then he thinks for a minute.

"The water was a relief! I was cooler for a while and some of the soot had washed off. My clothes didn't catch fire from the ashes as easily for a little while," Dad says and looks over at Mom who has tears runnin' down her face. "Then we climbed back up the hill and picked up where we left off; finding tools the firestorm had not burned up. I had taken my shovel with me to the water, so I had one to use again. Others weren't so lucky and after finding an ax or shovel, quickly dropped them, because the tools were still mighty hot or the handles were burned off altogether."

"Weren't you scared?" I asked. I had gone cold from hearing his story and my heart was thumping in my chest. The smell of smoke seemed to get stronger around Dad as he talked.

"Well, yes! . . . Yes, I was. But I still had to do what I had to do, to save myself and to continue to fight the fire. If we didn't get the fire out, we would all lose our homes," Dad answered solemnly. "Besides, being scared ain't nothin'. Everybody gets scared. It's what you do, even when you're scared, that matters."

He continued to talk about the forest—where it was that he fought the fire and how it looked after it burned, and he shared his sadness about the massive damage.

We've been to those places Dad's talking about. They were beautiful and now they are destroyed. Dad was also scared. As strong as he is, he was still really scared. But he said that isn't what matters. It's okay to be scared. It's what you do that counts.

"But, Dad, the forest is black and dead now. How will the birds and animals live there? There's no food left for them," Betty asked. "I'm worried about the animals. How will they survive?"

"Well now, I can see how that might be a concern. You know, there is more food left in the forest than you know. Right now, if you walked through the forest, it would look like a big charcoal drawing—mostly black and gray. But there is still plenty of life in there. There are beetles, called the black fire beetle, that eat the dead wood and lay their eggs in burned trees. And the black-headed woodpecker, among some other birds, like to eat those same beetles. Some plants are opportunistic and will germinate and sprout in the areas where the sun can reach now that the trees are dead. Heck, next year we'll go morel hunting and have us a mushroom feast!"[21] He almost laughed at that. Then Dad took a sip of his coffee and continued.

As I listen to Dad, my heart hurts with love for him and for our family. He says that even with a devastating fire, the forest can come back even stronger. That is how it is for me too—that I am now stronger somehow.

"The pine cones of the lodgepole pine tree don't even open and release their seeds until the resin is burned away, so they need the fire to germinate. Even though the forest has burned, it will come back again. Actually, some of it is still burning. The forest rangers and firefighters will get the fire completely out in another couple of days." He looked at Mom and Aunt Dolly when he said this.

Aunt Dolly piped up as Dad took a couple bites of his meal. "Well, our forest is made of mostly ponderosa pine. It is a tree that has very thick bark to survive surface fires. Another ponderosa pine defense is self-pruning branches. The lower branches wither and drop off to keep the higher branches alive and above most fires. Even the buds and needles have defenses against the fire."[22]

"Let's hope a lot of them survived. This was one wild, raging fire," Dad says. "So, the forest will revive, and the towns will too." He reported that the evacuation has been reversed and residents of Deadwood could head back to their houses to check for damage. Some folks were waiting for the fire to be completely out. There was still a lot of smoke in Deadwood and in neighboring towns.

"Some folks will leave instead of rebuilding," Dad says in a sad voice.

"Yet, we are so, so thankful that our home was

spared and that you are back safe and sound," Aunt Dolly says with tears in her eyes. She goes over to Dad and kisses her brother's cheek. Her lips carry away some of the fire's soot.

"Well, now. I suppose you are just ready to drop. You kids let Dad finish his meal. Then, Bill, you can take a shower to get that soot off and get some rest, for heaven's sake," Mom says with a catch in her voice. She wipes her eyes with her apron and refills Dad's coffee cup. Everyone sits around the table and on the floor near Dad. Then he finishes his meal while we all just sit around gazing at him.

I have such a large lump in my throat I can't even swallow. I don't know how to share that there has been a change inside me. I feel more confident in myself, but I cannot be sure how to say it so I stay quiet. I know now that it's okay to be scared. That gives me hope that I can be scared but also brave at the same time.

Our family has survived this forest fire and the complications that have come, over the last couple of days. I'm confident that we'll be able to survive whatever comes, in the future.

Epilogue

On Friday, Aunt Jolene and her three children returned to Deadwood. She told us about the drive out of town, the tree falling on a car near their car, and the explosion.

"The forest rangers were so brave. They dowsed that burning car and in a few minutes the fire was out. They used a big, two-man saw to cut that tree, then moved it over to clear the road. We all got turned around and finally drove out of that burning alley. What a scare, though!" she said. "We spent two nights in the Rapid City Armory. They had cots for sleeping and emergency food for us."

The back of their house was scorched, but other houses were burned down. The whole house smelled of smoke, and Aunt Jolene said it would take weeks to get the smell out.

Uncle Roger spent two weeks in the hospital, then returned to work "as good as new"—to quote Aunt Jolene.

The electricity was restored after a few days.

We had to eat up most of the food in the freezer and some things spoiled from the fridge, but Mom said this was a good opportunity to really clean the freezer before we started filling it up again.

Thousands of firefighters from surrounding city fire departments, forest rangers, Ellsworth Airforce Base, and a variety of out-of-state rangers, such as the Custer Indian Reservation rangers in Wyoming, Crow and Cheyenne Indian rangers from Billings, Montana, and Sioux Indian rangers from South Dakota, plus many volunteers who were untrained civilians from the Homestake Gold Mine and Highway Patrol officers, finally controlled the blaze.[23] It was one of the most devastating forest fires in the history of our state.

We were all so grateful that both Dad and Uncle Roger were healthy, as well as the other men and women who fought the forest fire. Over sixty structures in Deadwood burned, including the power and telephone lines, motels, construction businesses, and family homes. Some cattle died, but no human lives were lost,[24] and Mom said that was a blessing.

The mayor of Deadwood proclaimed Sunday to be a Day of Prayer in thanksgiving for our deliverance from the fire,[25] like it was God that did all the work, instead of Dad and lots of people like him. Still, we did our share of praying, so I s'pose God had something to do with it.

The next week, Dad drove our family through Deadwood to see where the fire had been. We visited our

PROCLAMATION

By the authority vested in me as
Mayor of the City of Deadwood,
County of Lawrence, State of South Dakota,
I hereby declare and proclaim
SUNDAY, SEPTEMBER 13, 1959
AS A DAY OF PRAYER
in thanksgiving to the Eternal Father of us all,
for our deliverance from a fire which
could have totally destroyed our city.
I humbly request that all the church bells be rung on
Sunday morning at 8 o'clock,
as a call to worship,
so that those people without church affiliation
may join with their fellow citizens in
an act of prayerful thanksgiving.

Attested: Glen Swanson, Auditor

cousins to see for ourselves where the fire burned their house. The entire back of their house was scorched to a dark brown and the trees behind the house were blackened. Later that month, we helped our cousins clean and repaint their house.

There was a big pancake breakfast in the town to thank the firefighters and volunteers.[26] A few weeks later in October, our family joined many others on the mountainside north of Deadwood to plant trees.

The next summer we went back to Ice Box Canyon with our cousins, Aunt Jolene, and Uncle Roger. It was one of our favorite picnic sites in the part of the forest that had been burned. In some areas the tops of the trees were green, and, in other places, the tops were burned but the lower branches looked okay. We were able see the trees, brush, and grasses returning.

"Look at all the flowers!" Betty said, and we girls stood and looked around, silently admiring the many flowers that we had never seen in these woods before.

Dad said, "See how the forest recovers from a fire? Fires can actually be a good thing, because the burned wood and foliage create nutrients for new plants. There will be more sunlight until the trees leaf out again. That sunlight will provide a chance for new trees to grow as well."

Dad's words made me think. I knew that if nature could recover from such a crisis, so could I.

The forest recovers from a fire.

Deadwood Fire of 1959
Statistics[27]

- 1,000—Firefighters fighting the fire within the first hour
- 3,600—Firefighters plus volunteers fighting the fire by sundown the first day
- 27—Bulldozers used to fight the fire
- 4—Air tankers called to fight the fire
- 96 degrees—Temperature outside when the fire started
- 36—Hours that the evacuation period lasted
- 4,501—Acres burned in the fire
- 60—Structures destroyed in the fire
- $1.5M—Damage caused by the fire (amount in 1959)

The loss of more than 60 structures, including two lumber plants inside the city limits and at least seven homes, made the fire one of the most-costly in the state's history.[28] In addition, because so many families left the area, there was substantial permanent job loss and economic downturn. "The 1959 fire consumed 4500 acres and cost the city $3 million by the time it was extinguished." (1959 Deadwood Fire photo caption)

"The Deadwood Fire of 1959 remains to this day the most destructive fire to private property, homes and infrastructure ever recorded in South Dakota,"[29] according to Jerome F. Harvey, (Jerome Harvey's son) who presented information about the blaze at a "National Fire Protection Association World Safety Conference and Exposition in 2003."

Endnotes

1 **Pg. 4**, Lead schools were evacuated at the same time-*"Deadwood's schools were quickly dismissed and businesses closed as the town of nearly 4,000 was evacuated."* From: **'Fire Was in the Air' in Deadwood 60 Years Ago,** by Jim Holland, Journal Staff, Rapid City Journal, Sep. 16, 2019.

2 **Pg. 21**, *"The fire started about one o'clock in a trash burner, behind the Hillcrest Manor in Central City, on Highway 14A."* From *"Souvenir Edition, The Deadwood Forest Fire: Black Hills Holocaust of 1959."* And **Incinerator at Hillcrest Manor Sets Holocaust**, the Black Hills Weekly, Wed. Sep. 16, 1959.

3 **Pg. 21**, *"Fire and rescue squads from Deadwood are fighting the blaze behind the Hillcrest Manor. The fire company has been called from Lead, as well. Other fire squads are also being called from the towns of Spearfish, Custer, and Sturgis. The Forest Service has set up a fire checkpoint on Main Street in Deadwood, in front of the Franklin Hotel. Recruits from Ellsworth Air Base have joined the fight."* From: **Locals Recall Deadwood Fire of '59,** by Deb Holland, Journal Staff, Rapid City Journal, Sep. 7, 2009.

4 **Pg. 22**, *"It has been forty-two days without rain and today's temperature of 96-degrees holds no hope for any rain. And . . . I am sorry to say there is no rain forecasted for the near future."* From: *"Souvenir Edition, The Deadwood Forest Fire: Black Hills Holocaust of 1959."*

5 **Pg. 22**, *"The fire has just recently jumped Highway 385. Those living in Central City and Deadwood should begin to evacuate, especially you folks on the east side. Other folks in nearby towns get ready to go in case the fire spreads in your direction, as well."* From: **September 8, 1959!** *"Souvenir Edition, The Deadwood Forest Fire: Black Hills Holocaust of 1959."*

6 **Pg. 22**, *"Residents were routed 'through Lower Main Street toward Sturgis,'"* From: **Worst Holocaust in Northern Hills in 80 Years is Believed Controlled,** by Winnifred Lindstrom, Deadwood Pioneer Times, Wed. Sep. 9, 1959. Downloaded on Jan. 20, 2020 at https://bhpioneer.newspapers.com/image/93274103.

7 **Pg. 36**, *"'Harry Anthony Daniels, owner and deejay of KDSJ,' who is the radio announcer. Following his stint in the Army during World War II, Harry moved with his brother to Deadwood where the radio station was started in 1947. The radio station has stayed in the hands of the Daniels brothers for 35 years."* From: **HARRY ANTHONY DANIELS, August, 6, 1918 to September 5, 2020**, City of Deadwood, archives@deadwood.com found at: http://www.deadwoodcenturyawards.com/wall/daniels.shtml.

8 **Pg. 41**, *Lawrence County State's Attorney William H. Carnahan manned the phone lines in Sheriff McGrath's office.* From: **Sherrif's Office is Command Post in Frenzied Battle Against Fire**, Rapid City Journal, Wed. Sept. 9, 1959, Pg.2.

9 **Pg. 59**, *"The miners from the Homestake Gold Mine have been called to join the forest rangers and firefighters to battle the blaze."* From: **'Fire Was in the Air' in Deadwood 60 Years Ago,** by Jim Holland, Journal Staff, Rapid City Journal, Sep. 16, 2019. And from: **South Dakota and Surrounding States Aid Deadwood Fight Fire,** by Camille Yuill, Black Hills Weekly, September 16, 1959. Downloaded on Jan. 20, 2020 from: Deadwood Pioneer-Times (Deadwood, South Dakota), Wed. Sept. 9 1959, Pg. 1 at: https://bhpioneer.newspapers.com/image/93274103.

10 **Pg. 60**, *". . . over 3,600 volunteers, foresters and firefighters working to put out this fire. Homes and businesses in Deadwood are burning and it looks like a battle zone."* From: **Locals Recall Deadwood Fire of '59,** by Deb Holland, Journal Staff, Rapid City Journal, Sep. 7, 2009.

11 **Pg. 60**, *"Pastors of churches, off-duty police, doctors, nurses and their spouses, professional men and school girls will be working in shifts to feed the firefighters and provide a spot for the men to rest. These volunteers are camped out at the Franklin Hotel, which has become the headquarters for the rescue operation."* From: **Miners, Youngsters, -Everybody Joins War Against Flames,** by Ken Jumper, Rapid City Journal Staff Writer, Sep. 9, 1959.

12 **Pg. 78**, *"The men each have white bandages wrapped around heads or limbs. Uncle Roger is lying on a stretcher."* - In fact, very few people got injured, however, "Two National Guardsmen were seriously burned when the fire overtook their bulldozers while fighting the fire." From: **'Fire Was in the Air' in Deadwood 60 Years Ago,** by Jim Holland, Journal Staff, Sep. 16, 2019 reported "There were injuries, but no fatalities" and **Deadwood Fire remembered 60 Years Later,** by Jim Holland Journal Staff, Sep. 16, 2019, taken from the world wide web on April 9, 2020 at 10:53 pm at: https://rapidcityjournal.com/news/local/deadwood-fire-remembered-years-later/article_3b4546c6-c6b2-57a1-bdf2-42319c559f07.html.

13 **Pg. 78**, *"The National Guard has joined with helicopters that are dropping a slurry called bentonite on the hot spots."* From: **Deadwood Fire Remembered 60 Years Later,** by Jim Holland Journal Staff, Sep. 16, 2019, taken from the world wide web on April 9, 2020 at 10:53 pm at: https://rapidcityjournal.com/news/local/deadwood-fire-remembered-years-later/article_3b4546c6-c6b2-57a1-bdf2-42319c559f07.html.

14 **Pg. 84**, *". . .Highway 385, leading to Custer, Hill City, and Hot Springs has been cut off."* From: **September 8th,**

1959! Souvenir Edition: The Deadwood Forest Fire, Black Hills Holocaust of 1959.

15 **Pg. 86**, *"Governor Ralph Herseth has ordered seven National Guard units from around the Black Hills into action. He also contacted the Governors Hickey of Wyoming and Davis of North Dakota for assurance of national help if needed. The American Red Cross is providing food and a make-shift resting place for weary firefighters at the courthouse."* From: **South Dakota and Surrounding States Aid Deadwood Fight Fire,** by Camille Yuill, Black Hills Weekly, September 16, 1959. Downloaded on Jan. 20, 2020 from: Deadwood Pioneer-Times (Deadwood, South Dakota), Wed. Sept. 9 1959, Pg. 1 at: https://bhpioneer.newspapers.com/image/93274103.

16 **Pg. 86**, *"Patients have been moved to the Homestake Hospital in Lead."* "All patients at St. Joseph's Hospital were taken by ambulance and private cars either to the Homestake Hospital in Lead or transferred to private homes in adjoining cities, depending on the seriousness of their illness." From: **Worst Holocaust in Northern Hills In 80 Years Is Believed Controlled,** by Winnifred Lindstrom, Deadwood Pioneer Times, Wed. Sep. 9, 1959. Downloaded on Jan 20, 2020 at: https://bhpioneer.newspapers.com/image/93274103.

17 **Pg. 96**, *"Lead will most likely not have to evacuate. The fire is 80% contained."* "For many hours after the first alarm was sounded the city of Lead, home of the Homestake Gold Mine, was considering evacuation. By midnight this September 8th the residents of Lead were told they would be able to remain." From: **September 8,1959!** Souvenir Edition, The Deadwood Forest Fire: Black Hills Holocaust of 1959.

18 **Pg. 129**, *"They also serve who only sit and wait."* This is a mis-quote from John Milton's **Sonnet 19: When I Consider How My Light is Spent**, From: https://www.poetryfoundation.org/poems/44750/sonnet-19-when-i-consider-how-my-light-is-spent.

19 **Pg. 145**, *"The fire isn't out yet. Not by a long shot. It'll probably take a couple more weeks for workers to get it*

all out and that's if we get some help from mother nature." In fact, the fire was finally considered out on September 23rd. From: **Fire Danger 95 . . . Temperature 96 . . . Wind 13 Miles Per Hour . . . 42 Days and No Rain . . . .** , Souvenir Edition, The Deadwood Forest Fire: Black Hills Holocaust of 1959."

20 **Pg. 149**, *"I saw the firestorm dancing on the water and I held my breath for as long as I could, and then some!"* Dad is relating his story of laying down in Little Strawberry Creek as reported by Jerome Harvey, a longtime Deadwood resident and volunteer firefighter. From: **Locals Recall Deadwood Fire of '59**, by Deb Holland, Rapid City Journal Staff, Sep. 7, 2009.

21 **Pg. 151**, *". . .there is more food left in the forest than you know. Right now, if you walked through the forest, it would look like a big charcoal drawing—mostly black and gray. But there is still plenty of life in there. There are beetles (the black fire beetle) that eat the dead wood and lay their eggs in the burned trees. And the black-headed woodpecker, among some other birds, likes to eat those same beetles. Some plants are opportunistic and will germinate and sprout in the areas where the sun can reach now that the trees are dead. Heck, next year we'll go morel hunting and have us a mushroom feast!"* From: **The Charcoal Forest: How Fire Helps Animals and Plants,** by Beth A. Peluso, Mountain Press Publishing Co., Missoula, MT. 2007, Pg. 120.

22 **Pg. 152**, *"Our forest is made of mostly ponderosa pine. It is a tree that has very thick bark to survive surface fires. Another ponderosa pine defense is self-pruning branches. The lower branches wither and drop off to keep the higher branches alive and above most fires. Even the buds and needles have defenses against the fire."* From: **The Charcoal Forest: How Fire Helps Animals and Plants,** by Beth A. Peluso, Mountain Press Publishing Co., Missoula, MT. 2007.

23 **Pg. 156**, *"Thousands of firefighters, many of whom were untrained civilian volunteers and miners from Lead's Homestake Gold Mine, finally controlled the blaze a week later."* From: **South Dakota and Surrounding States Aid Deadwood**

Fight Fire, by Camille Yuill, Black Hills Weekly, September 16, 1959. Downloaded on Jan. 20, 2020 from: Deadwood Pioneer-Times (Deadwood, South Dakota), Wed. Sept. 9 1959, Pg. 1 at: https://bhpioneer.newspapers.com/image/93274103.

24 **Pg. 156,** *"Over sixty structures in Deadwood have burned, including the power and telephone lines, motels, construction businesses, and family homes. Some cattle have died, but no human lives were lost."* From: **Locals Recall Deadwood Fire of '59,** by Deb Holland, Rapid City Journal Staff, Sep. 7, 2009.

25 **Pg. 156,** *"Mayor proclaims a Day of Prayer of thanksgiving."* From: **Million Dollar Forest Fire Mop-up Starts**, Deadwood Pioneer, September 11, 1959.

26 **Pg. 157,** *"About a month after the fire, we had this big pancake feed to thank the firefighters,"* From: **Locals Recall Deadwood Fire of '59** By Deb Holland, Journal Staff, Sep. 7, 2009, Rapid City Journal.

27 **Pg. 160,** Statistics from: **Historic Wildfire in the Black Hills,** by Jerome F. Harvey, and **Fire Danger 95. . . Temperature 96. . .Wind 13 Miles Per Hour. . .42 Days And No Rain. . . .** , Souvenir Edition, The Deadwood Forest Fire, Black Hills Holocaust of 1959.

28 **Pg. 160,** *"Total damages exceeded $1.5 million, or $13.7 million in today's dollars,"* From: **'Fire Was in the Air' in Deadwood 60 Years Ago,** by Jim Holland, Rapid City Journal Staff, Sep. 16, 2019.

29 **Pg. 161,** *"The Deadwood Fire of 1959 remains to this day the most destructive fire to private property, homes and infrastructure ever recorded in South Dakota, . . ."* From: **Locals Recall Deadwood Fire of '59,** by Deb Holland, Journal Staff, Sep. 7, 2009, Rapid City Journal.

Bibliography

Newspaper staff writer. (Thursday, September 10, 1959). "Northern Hills Forest Fire Still Critical" and secondary column, titled: "Hot Spots, Winds, Lower Humidity "Harass" Weary Fire Line Fighters". Lead Daily Call, Col, 66, NO. 25. Downloaded from the world wide web on January 20, 2020 from https://www.newspapers.com/image/93668012

Newspaper staff writer. (September 9,1959)."Huge Forest Blaze Threatens Deadwood", Deadwood Pioneer Times, Vol. 84, NO 79, United Press International.

Camille Yuill, (September 9, 1959). "South Dakota and Surrounding States Aid Deadwood Fight Fire" Deadwood Pioneer Times, Vol. 84, NO 79, United Press International.

Camille Yuill. (September 9, 1959)."Nat'l Forest Flies in Aid to Fight Fire". Deadwood Pioneer Times, Vol. 84, NO 79, United Press International.

Jim Holland, Journal Staff. (September 16, 2019). "Evidence of 1959 fires still visible". Rapid City Journal. Taken from the world wide web on January 20, 2020 at 5:00 pm at: https://rapidcityjournal.com/news/local/evidence-of-deadwood-fire-still-visible/article_ec266b65-bc14-572d-a54e-b61692de92e6.html

"Million Dollar Forest Fire Mop-up Starts," Deadwood Pioneer Times, Friday, September 11, 1959. Page one and Page 6. Taken from the world wide web on January

19, 2020 at: https://bhpioneer.newspapers.com/image/93274174

Winnifred Lindstrom, (Wednesday, September 16, 1959). "Worst Holocaust in Northern Hills In 80 Years Believed Controlled". The Black Hills Weekly (Deadwood, South Dakota), Page 2. Printed on Jan 20, 2020 from the world wide web at: https://www.newspapers.com/image/95456622

Deb Holland, Journal Staff. (September 7, 2009). "Locals recall Deadly Fire of 1959". Rapid City Journal.

"Deadwood marks 60th anniversary of Fire of '59," By Jaci Conrad Pearson, Black Hills Pioneer, September 9, 2019.

"Early Fire Scenes of Disastrous Blaze," The Black Hills Weekly (Deadwood, South Dakota). Wednesday, September 16,1959—Page 3.

"Incinerator at Hillcrest Manor Sets Holocaust" The Black Hills Weekly (Deadwood, South Dakota) Wed, Sep 16, 1959. Page 1. From: https://www.newspapers.com/image/95456628 Downloaded on Jan 20, 2020.

The Deadwood Forest Fire Souvenir Edition of SMOKEY (1959). About the Black Hills Holocaust of 1959. City of Deadwood.

Kathy Furgang. (2006). National Geographic Kids: Wildfires (ages 5-13). National Geographic.

Beth Al. Peluso. (2007).The Charcoal Forest: How Fire Helps Animals and Plants (ages 5-13) Mountain Press Publishing.

William H. Cottrell Jr. (1989) The Book of Fire! (ages 9-99). Mountain Press Publishing Company.

Seymour Simon, (April 2016). Wildfires. Harper Collins Publishers.

Mark Thiessen. (August 2016). Extreme Wildfire: Smoke Jumpers, High-Tech Gear, Survival Tactics, and the Extraordinary Science of Fire. National Geographic.

Michael L. Cooper (March 2014.) Fighting Fire!: Ten of the Deadliest Fires in American History and How We Fought Them. Henry Hold and Company.

Interviews

Conversations between Annette (Stabnow) Gagliardi and Elizabeth (Stabnow) Glaser about eyewitness accounts of the Deadwood Fire of 1959, August 12, 2019. Elizabeth's contact: flizg2016@yahoo.com.

Conversations between Annette (Stabnow) Gagliardi and Cathy (Stabnow) Rufer about eyewitness accounts of the Deadwood Fire of 1959, February 12, 2020. Cathy's contact: Honeylady50@msn.com.

Josh and Lynsey Tjaden. Personal communication about firefighters and their equipment, November 10, 2015, November 27, 2015, January 1, 2016, February 21, 2016, May 15, 2016 and February 13, 2020. Contact: ltjaden35@gmail.com.

Nick Caple. Personal communication on November 25, 2015, December 10, 2015, and February 18, 2020. Contact: nicolas_caple@hotmail.com.

Photo & Map

1. Family photo from Bill and Anne Stabnow and Dolly (Stabnow) Hemmah archives.
2. Area Map reproduced by Elizabeth A. Glaser

Illustrations by Elizabeth A. Glaser:
1. Ponderosa Pine
2. Harry Daniels in studio
3. Men running to Strawberry Creek
4. Deer & wolf running towards Dad
5. New sapling in burned forest
6. Burn barrel and yard where fire began
7. Annette in the pine tree (cover)

Ponderosa Pines
Days of the Deadwood Forest Fire

Annette Gagliardi is a Minnesota teacher, author, and poet. Her first full-length poetry book, *A Short Supply of Viability,* was released in July of 2022. Annette has authored two children's books: *The Three Betty Goats Griff,* and *Resourceful Erica.* Her poetry appears in *Motherwell, Wisconsin Review, American Diversity Report, Origami Poems Project, Door IS Ajar,* and many more online and in-print magazines.

Find more of Annette's work at:
https://annette-gagliardi.com/

Illustrator, Elizabeth Glaser, is retired and lives in northern Wisconsin with her husband. Most of her artwork is of animals and landscapes that reflect her love of nature. She has worked in oils, acrylics, colored pencils, and graphite. Elizabeth is self-taught, but has taken independent art and painting, and commercial art classes. In addition to drawing most of her life, crafting has always been an interest, and includes greeting cards, scrapbooking, quilting, and wood art. While earning a living as a secretary in numerous capacities and raising two children, Elizabeth occasionally took part in art shows and gallery sales. Most of her artwork sales have been by commission. More recently, she has illustrated six children's picture books, including two with author, Annette Gagliardi: *The Three Betty Goats Griff,* and *Resourceful Erica. Ponderosa Pines* is Elizabeth's first illustrated chapter book.

Erica Onsrud, Ponderosa Pines' cover layout designer, is a creative collaborator and mentor who uses her experience in strategic thinking, storytelling, and design to bring ideas to life. Erica is fueled by curiosity, adventures in the outdoors, and strawberry-rhubarb jam. She lives in Minneapolis.

CPSIA information can be obtained
at www.ICGtesting.com
Printed in the USA
JSHW022313131122
33135JS00001B/6

CPSIA information can be obtained
at www.ICGtesting.com
Printed in the USA
JSHW022313131122
33135JS00001B/6

9 781955 338073